# FIGHTING FOR REESE

Redemption Harbor Security Series

# Katie Reus

Copyright © 2024 by Katie Reus®. All rights reserved.

Cover art by Sweet 'N Spicy Designs
Editor: Julia Ganis
Proofreader: Book Nook Nuts
Author website: www.katiereus.com

This book is a work of fiction. The names, characters, places, and incidents are products of the writer's imagination and are not to be construed as real. Any resemblance to persons, living or dead, actual events, locales or organizations is entirely coincidental. All rights reserved. With the exception of quotes used in reviews, this book may not be reproduced or used in whole or in part by any means existing without written permission from the author.

Also, thank you for not sharing your copy of this book. This purchase allows you one legal copy for your own personal reading enjoyment on your personal computer or device. You do not have the right to resell, distribute, print or transfer this book, in whole or in part, to anyone, in any format, via methods either currently known or yet to be invented, or upload this book to a file sharing program. If you would like to share this book with another person, please purchase an additional copy for each person you share it with. Thank you for respecting the author's work.

# Dedication

*For my sister, who deserves all the good things.*

# Chapter 1

If Reese had ever been the type of girl to imagine what a dream wedding would look like, it would have been at this gorgeous greenhouse and surrounding botanical gardens. It didn't matter that it was the beginning of February, everything in this giant greenhouse was lush with color and the atmosphere was perfect thanks to whatever kind of temperature regulation they had going on. The sky and stars were visible above them through the glass ceilings, and as her best friend finished her vows to the man she'd waited years for, Reese wiped away a few stray tears.

She wasn't a crier, but seeing two people so absolutely right for each other link their lives together... Well, apparently she was a teeny bit of a closet romantic.

When she briefly caught the eye of Constantine Pierce—aka Cash to everyone who knew him—she quickly averted her gaze. But she couldn't actually avoid him, not when he was the best man and she was the maid of honor. Oh crap, the vows were over and it was time to follow the bride and groom down the aisle. Which meant walking directly next to Mr. smells-so-good-I-want-to-lick-him-all-over. *Gah!*

Moving quickly, she fell in step with Cash, who gave her a sideways look she couldn't, or didn't *want* to, define. Because of course he was smiling.

The gorgeous man with the electric green eyes was *always* smiling. It was ridiculous.

"I never took you for a crier," he murmured as the live quartet played "Moon River" while they walked down the aisle, the rest of the bridal party behind them.

"I have allergies." She sniffed imperiously but kept a perfect smile in place for the photographer as they passed by. "These aren't tears."

"Ah, okay. Well, you look beautiful tonight. In case no one has told you, I wanted to make sure you know."

She blinked, wondering what his game was. But she simply said, "Thanks. You look very nice too."

He snickered slightly and murmured something about his ego, but she couldn't be sure because the entire bridal party had piled out into the courtyard behind the mansion-sized greenhouse. It was chilly now that they were outside and she wrapped her arms around herself—only for Cash to drape his jacket around her.

"Oh... thanks," she whispered because the wedding planner was shushing all of them. Would it be totally weird if she buried her face in the lapels and smelled it? Hmm. She'd do it later when no one was looking.

"All right everyone." Jasmine, the wedding planner who'd whipped together a wedding in a single month, held up an elegant hand for the big wedding party. "The ceremony was beautiful, and huge congrats to the two of you," she said, smiling warmly at Hailey and Jesse. "But if you're going to do the dance at the reception, we need to hustle so you can avoid getting stopped by guests."

"Everyone listen to Jasmine," Hailey called out to the group but didn't take her eyes off Jesse. Nope, her bestie was looking up at her new husband with actual stars in her eyes.

And everyone else was standing around, not quite listening, while Reese could see the guests starting to move toward the exit. Uh oh, their window was closing.

Reese looked up at Cash who nodded at her, as if he read her mind.

"Come on Rowan, Easton, let's go." Cash started herding them while Reese motioned to three others.

"Let's go, let's go," she snapped, using her "work" voice.

Everyone lined up neatly and followed as she continued ordering them.

Jasmine fell in next to Reese as they brought up the tail end, quite literally herding them toward the giant garden maze like tipsy cats. "It's like everyone has had a glass of champagne and just forgets to listen."

"More like three glasses each," Reese murmured, snickering. "Not that I've had any." She'd been drinking only water, wanting to be the best maid of honor *ever* tonight. But as soon as Jesse and Hailey took off on their honeymoon, she was letting loose.

Jasmine laughed lightly as the whole group stepped into the first entrance of the maze.

Sure, this whole thing was a little over-the-top but these two were only getting married once. And why the hell not go over-the-top for your wedding? It was Hailey's day and she was going to get what she wanted.

Jasmine let out a short whistle that got everyone quiet—except Hailey and Jesse, who were currently making out.

Reese fell in step with Cash because they'd be entering the maze together in just a few moments. She slid off his jacket, only subtly smelling it before she handed it over.

"Everyone, we've practiced this half a dozen times but I've got little lights and arrows pointing you in the right direction. You all have eight minutes to make it to your places. Can I trust everyone to do that?"

"Yes! And we're going to beat all of you!" Skye, who was one of their bosses, and super competitive, grabbed Rowan's arm and dragged him past one of the hedges.

Reese looked up at Cash and shook her head. "It's not like it matters who gets there first. We all enter at the same time."

"So what? Let's kick her ass." Now he linked his arm through hers, and despite her desire to keep her distance from the annoyingly cheerful and gorgeous man, she found herself laughing as she raced along with him.

With no heating lamps in the maze, their breath was visible in front of them as they ran, but she barely felt the chill anymore. And sure enough, there were arrows and cute little signs pointing them in the right direction until they reached the end of their portion of the maze.

In the center of the maze was a stunning garden where the actual reception would be taking place. Hailey had got it into her head—thanks to a suggestion from Cash—that they should all dance into the reception from different parts of the maze, kicking off the reception in style.

And okay, the idea was kick-ass and so much fun that Reese had fallen in love with it too. So once the guests were all seated—they didn't have to enter through a maze; there was a single main entrance for everyone else—the twelve people from the bridal party and the bride and groom would dance into the reception area as a Whitney Houston song blasted from the speakers and balloons were strategically freed around the area.

"We totally beat them," she gasped out as they reached their waiting spot. Then she pulled her cell phone out of her flowers. "With time to spare." She texted Skye quickly with an emoji of a woman running.

"Yeah we did." Cash peeked around the hedge. "Man, Jasmine has this thing under control. I feel like she'd be a great drill sergeant. Just hotter."

Reese narrowed her gaze at his back, annoyed at the small spike of jealousy that punched through her. But she quickly shelved it. She didn't care if he thought Jasmine was hot—the woman was. Tall, with gorgeous, Disney princess style thick hair that fell down her back in waves and a Jessica Rabbit type body, yep, the woman was beyond stunning. It just annoyed her that Cash had noticed.

"Hey, I have a weird request," Reese said as he ducked back behind the hedge. They still had three minutes before the music was supposed to start.

"Anything."

She blinked as he looked down at her with those startling green eyes she still wasn't used to. Because when he pinned her with his stare, it was as if the world fell away to only the two of them. "You don't even know what I'm going to ask. It could be something really weird."

He lifted a big shoulder, and oh god, he looked good enough to eat in that tux. Which had to be custom-made given his big arms. *Ugh.* She hated that she found his biceps so mouthwatering. No wonder his jacket had been so big on her.

"I'm open to weird."

*Of course he is.* She laughed and held out her phone. "I want to take a selfie with you and send it to my mom to get her off my back. She heard you were my date at that gala back in December and has been asking about you ever since." In fact, her mother had been texting her nonstop about Cash, and that wasn't like her mom. Both her parents were limited on the communication. Until recently. "She knows you're the best man tonight too." Because it was all over social media that billionaire Jesse Lennox was marrying his childhood sweetheart.

Jesse's PR team had been leaking select information about the upcoming nuptials and an "inside source" had let it leak that the two of them had known each other since they were teens and had kept in touch while Hailey was in Afghanistan. Considering all the shit in the news the last few years, their getting married was small potatoes, but Jesse had been insistent on controlling the narrative. He never wanted Hailey's privacy breached so he'd done what he did best—taken control.

And Reese respected the hell out of that.

To her surprise, Cash leaned in easily next to her as she held her phone out, not even questioning the selfie. She snapped one, then said, "Okay, one more just in case." And as she snapped the picture, he turned and kissed her cheek.

Despite herself, she felt her cheeks warm at the small intimacy, but she laughed it off. "Do you care if I send both to her? This should get her off my back for a few months about who I'm dating." And Reese would definitely not be making that adorable picture her screen saver. *Nope.*

"Don't care at all. If you want, I'll show up to a family dinner and propose in front of your parents."

She stared up at him in horror right as the music started.

"That's our cue!" He hustled her out with him, and as they danced out into the reception where the rest of the two hundred guests waited, and she knew she'd remember this night forever.

Surrounded by her favorite people in the world, and directly next to a man she was totally *not* harboring an inappropriate crush on, this was one of her favorite nights ever.

# Chapter 2

Cash tossed his cards onto the table, grinning across it at Reese, who simply scrunched her nose, made annoyed sounds, then threw her cards facedown.

"Apparently poker is not my game," she grumbled.

"Or more likely, Cash is cheating." Easton grinned at Reese as he leaned back in his chair.

Hailey and Jesse, two of his childhood best friends, had left half an hour ago on their honeymoon—to be spent in Paris and other parts of France and Europe for the next month. So the majority of the bridal party had reconvened back in the greenhouse where the actual ceremony had taken place. There were string lights everywhere, the mood of the lighting romantic and almost magical. A couple fountains offered a soothing bubbling background in addition to the light classical music being pumped in from somewhere.

"Hey." He tossed a cashew at Easton's face. "Not cool!"

"Wait, are you really cheating?" Reese, all gorgeous indignation, stood up sans heels—which she'd lost about twenty minutes ago. She was petite, but curvy and all attitude. And in a crimson dress that wrapped around her like a second skin, her jet-black hair falling over her shoulders in waves since she'd pulled all the pins out earlier, she was his walking fantasy come to life. He hadn't even known he'd had one until she'd rolled into his life after driving his car as if she'd stolen it. She was occasionally surly, which he found ridiculously hot. Though everything she did he found hot. He'd been trying to needle her earlier by calling Jasmine attractive and he'd seen a small reaction from her.

"No, of course not," he said.

Easton snorted loudly.

And even Rowan, the traitor, shrugged. "Could be, he's a sneaky one."

"I'm not cheating!"

"Hmmm." Reese moved over next to him, pushing Rowan aside and stealing his chair as she looked at Cash intently. Then she burst out giggling and leaned in, her dark hair falling on him. "I'm cheating too. I'm just bad at it."

Jesus, this woman had him wrapped around her finger and didn't even realize it. He wanted to lean in and bury his face against her neck, simply inhale her, but was pretty sure he'd get a well-deserved palm across the face for it.

She snagged his glass of champagne, crossed her legs, and leaned back in her new chair as if she owned the place. "I think I'm done with poker anyway. Who wants to get in a few more dances before the night is over? Easton, that hot bartender was eyeing you earlier. Maybe you should get his number?"

Easton's cheeks tinged pink at Reese's abrupt change in subject, but he simply shook his head.

"Fine, I'll get it for you. Then I'm dancing."

"I'll dance with you...if you can keep up." Cash slung an arm around her shoulders, and to his surprise she leaned into him, still giggling. Normally she was so serious and a little grumpy with him, but tonight she'd let her hair down. Literally and figuratively. And he was so here for it. There were a hell of a lot of facets to this woman and he wanted to know all of them.

"This is the best champagne I've ever had," she said as they headed out of the greenhouse.

"Same." He scooped up her discarded heels by one of the fountains and crouched down to help her slide them on.

"You really are the nicest." The way she said it was almost accusing as she looked down at him.

And he wondered what it would be like for her to look down at him under very different circumstances. Naked ones. "Is that supposed to be a bad thing?"

"No, of course not. Just giving you a compliment, butthead."

"Butthead, really? We're back to that?"

"I've had a few glasses of champagne, so yes." She sniffed imperiously, sticking that pert little nose in the air before laughing again.

The sound was infectious, wrapping around him, making him lightheaded. He plucked his glass back from her, downed it before she could protest, then scooped her up in his arms as they headed to the dance floor.

To his surprise, she just laughed, the sound deep and throaty as he pulled her into his arms and held her close, moving to the fast-paced beat. Just as quickly, the song slowed, and even though he was very aware of all the guests on the dance floor around him, he could pretend it was just the two of them.

Him and Reese.

The snarky woman had gotten under his skin months ago when he'd first met her, and he was hooked.

"How much have you had to drink tonight?" he asked, wanting to know exactly where her head was at. Because she was looking at him with all the lust he felt—but no way in hell he'd ever take advantage of her.

"Enough to know what I want, but not enough to have regrets in the morning."

Oh hell, that was the perfect amount. He blinked and nearly stumbled at her answer, wondering if he was misunderstanding. Before he could respond, Jasmine was suddenly there, looking between the two of them, her expression pinched.

"I'm sorry to interrupt your dance, but I was hoping you could help with something?" she asked him.

"Ah..." *No!* He didn't want to help. He wanted to keep dancing with Reese, to lose himself with her tonight. But he couldn't actually say that. Right?

"Oh, it's fine." Reese stepped away from him and whatever spell that had woven around them shattered. "I see Skye about to head out with Colt so I'm going to say goodbye. I'll see you before the end of the night though." But her words were dismissive and he got the feeling she was going to avoid him again.

Sighing to himself, he gave Jasmine a neutral smile. "What's going on?"

"Well...Rowan is sort of getting into it with someone. A woman. And he's been so polite the last few rehearsals that it's taken me by surprise. He's being an asshole and I can't read if it will escalate or not. I don't think he's drinking but—"

*Rowan?* What the hell was going on? Alarmed, he fell in step with Jasmine. "Where is he?"

She motioned for him to follow and they exited the reception in the middle of the maze, taking the direct path straight out to find...yep, Rowan was towering over a lean redhead in a floor-length, backless gown.

The majority of guests were at the reception and some of the wedding party was still playing poker, but these two were outside the kitchen the caterers had been moving in and out of all night. And clearly in the way given that a handful of servers were having to skirt around them carrying full trays.

"My man, what's going on?" he called out, glad when Jasmine hung back to let him handle whatever this was. He'd only known Rowan for a couple months, but the man had always been so level-headed, even jovial.

Rowan's head jerked up to look at him, and he blinked at Cash, looking as if he was coming out of a haze. The man had trimmed his beard for the wedding, but he still looked rough around the edges. And right now, he was clearly pissed.

When the redhead turned, he realized he knew her. He'd never seen her dressed like this, however. No, they'd only ever been in-country together. "Holy shit, Adalyn?"

She gave him a half smile, nodded, clearly not surprised to see him. "Cash."

"What...you know her?" Rowan demanded, looking at Cash as if he'd somehow betrayed him.

"Yeah. What the hell is going on?" He glanced over his shoulder and waved off Jasmine who gave him a relieved look and hurried off. "Because you're worrying Jasmine."

"Oh." Rowan looked guilty as he scrubbed a hand over his head, then down over his face.

"You guys good?" He focused on Adalyn. "Also, when did you get here and also, *how* are you here?" Because he doubted Adalyn Bonnevie had just shown up out of the blue, uninvited.

"My plane was delayed but I managed to see Hailey and her new husband off before they left." She gave a tired smile, and as he pulled her in for a hug, he could see the striking redhead was exhausted. But her grip was solid, much like the woman. She'd always had a clear head in dangerous situations.

"How do you know Hailey? And what's going on with you two?" Things he didn't care nearly as much about as returning to the dance floor and kissing Reese senseless. Then hauling her off to his place for a night—or week—in his bed.

"Ah...I know Hailey from the same place I know you. Different circumstances...ish." Adalyn gave a wry smile.

"Ohhh." Adalyn worked for the CIA—or she had. Last he'd heard, she'd quit, but he wasn't sure if that was true or just rumors. He'd had a lot going on the last couple months.

Rowan made a sound between a scoff and a grumble. "Yeah and no way she invited you—"

"You know what, Rowan? Shut your stupid mouth and leave me alone," she snarled to the tall man before she patted Cash on the shoulder. "I'll be at the bar if you want to catch up. If not, I've got your new number courtesy of Hailey. We'll meet up later."

He nodded, a bit dazed that his "before" life had collided with his present. Or his past, since Hailey was his childhood friend. Whatever. Didn't matter. He gave Rowan a hard look. "It's clear that Hailey invited her, so whatever your beef is, can you deal for the next hour or so? Because it'll be a really bad look if one of Hailey's coworkers—one of her *friends*, because you know she loves your ass—makes a scene."

Rowan's jaw tightened and he looked as if he wanted to argue, but he finally nodded before stalking in the direction of the greenhouse. Thankfully that was away from the bar.

"Thank god," Cash muttered before heading back to the reception to find that Reese was nowhere to be seen.

*Well, hell.*

\*\*\*

Reese quickly made her way away from the reception as she spoke to her mom. There was too much noise and music to hear otherwise.

"So, it seems like you're having a good time." Reese's mom's voice was smooth over the phone, but she didn't miss the tinge of excitement in her words.

Because one of her mom's goals was for Reese to get married and start popping out kids. But really, her mom wanted her to marry someone in her family's tax bracket—*gross*. Her mom had been pushing that, along with a bunch of other things since she was a kid. Reese had been sent to a boarding school at twelve, and had been expected to graduate with her master's then PhD in degrees of her parents' choice—economics specifically. But as soon as she'd turned eighteen, she'd done exactly what she wanted.

Part of that was thanks to a trust her grandparents had left her, but also academic scholarships. So she'd gotten dual degrees in business and computer science—not her parents' choice, but they'd actually been okay with her degrees in the end. Mainly because they'd assumed she'd meet someone in college, get married, and fall in line. Her mom had known she'd never go into lobbying—*double gross*—but she'd expected Reese to live by her parents' rules. To volunteer at charities, marry a husband of their choosing, attend a church of their choosing…and she'd carved an entirely different path with no regrets.

"Yeah, the wedding was beautiful. Everyone's had a great time." And a teeny, tiny, petty part of Reese knew that her mom was jealous that she'd been invited to one of the most talked about weddings of the year. As if she even cared about that. No, she was just happy for her best friend.

"So what is going on with you and Constantine Pierce?"

"Ah, Cash and I are friends." She didn't mention that he was now working with her at Redemption Harbor Security because (a) she wasn't sure if he was telling people and (b) she didn't like to remind her mom where she worked because if her mom asked questions, she usually had to lie.

"Really darling, *Cash*?"

"Everyone calls him that." She felt almost defensive of him in that moment.

Her mom sniffed, but only said, "Well, what kind of friends are you?"

"We're dating," she blurted, then cursed herself even though this was exactly what she'd planned to tell her mom before. Then she'd had that weird moment with Cash on the dance floor and things had started to feel all too real. As if...maybe they *could* be dating. As if maybe she *wanted* to date him. "And he said he wants to meet you guys."

*Oh my god, what is wrong with me! Shut up, shut up, shut up!* Her brain simply laughed at her.

"Oh, well, that is wonderful. He's a bit rough around the edges but it's true what they say about him. Everything he touches turns to gold. Not to mention he had a distinguished stint in the army. If he ever decided to run for office, he'd be a shoo-in for anything as long as there are no skeletons in his closet. And he loves to donate to good causes, something you know I believe strongly in."

*Uh huh.* Her mom and dad only believed in giving so they could get something in return. They were freaking lobbyists, something that was hard for her to swallow. Almost as bad as knowing that her parents' love was conditional. She'd realized that nugget when she'd been about fifteen and the knowledge had burrowed deep, carved out a hole in her chest that had never fully healed. Also, her mom sure seemed to have an opinion on Cash, seemed to know quite a bit about him. Reese shouldn't be surprised since her parents kept an ear to the ground on everyone, it felt like. But still, it was unsettling. "Yep. I sure do."

Reese breathed in the cold air as she strolled along one of the cobblestone walkways, careful where she stepped in her heels. She could hear the beat of the music in the distance, see the lights shining from behind the maze of hedges and in the main greenhouse.

"We'll have to set something up soon. Perhaps when your father and I are back in the States we can do dinner."

Reese hadn't even realized they were anywhere else, but that was fairly typical. Once upon a time she'd have asked for details, but for the most part she tried to keep her distance from her parents' lives. It hurt less that way when they canceled on her for the billionth time. Though something told her they wouldn't cancel if she set up a dinner with Cash. And *that* knowledge really cut deep. "Sure, hey, I've gotta go, they're about to cut the cake."

"Oh of course, we love you."

"Love you too." Sighing to herself, she tucked her phone away as she reached the end of the path and realized she was at the edge of the valet parking lot.

Instead of heading back the way she'd come, she decided to loop back through the parking lot since the ground was a lot flatter.

As she passed by a line of SUVs, she saw movement in one and...froze. It was someone's naked back. A man. And he was... Oh god, yep, people were having sex in one of the SUVs.

She froze again.

It was Cash's SUV.

*What the hell?*

Feeling nauseous but not wanting to get caught staring like some king of perv, she jerked back, nearly tripped, but righted herself before hurrying, her heels clicking across the pavement.

It was difficult when her dress was so snug, but she moved as quick as she could, only slowing as she reached the valet area. One of the men standing by the valet stand stepped toward her but she shook her head.

"I'm just out for a stroll, not ready to leave yet." She tried to smile but couldn't force her face to cooperate.

The young man nodded and smiled at her.

"Are you guys hungry? Do you want cake or something?" she continued even as her gut twisted.

His eyes lit up, but then he shook his head. "We're not really supposed to take food or anything."

"Is your boss here tonight?"

"Ah..." The woman working with him grinned and shook her head. "No."

"All right, well we'll just see what happens, then."

They both grinned at her as she hurried off, trying to get her emotions under control. The warmth hit her as she stepped into the main building where everyone had left their coats when they arrived. The kitchens were on one end, but there was a waiting area where some people were clearly warming up with hot cocoa while they took a break from dancing.

"Reese." Jasmine called out from across the seating area when she saw her, tucking her cell phone away. "I wondered where you'd gotten off to."

The strangest sense of relief punched through Reese to see Jasmine—who she'd thought maybe was getting a quickie with Cash, and was ridiculously glad he wasn't banging her. Still, he was screwing someone, and ugh, she absolutely couldn't think about that right now. *Nope, nope, nope.*

"Hey, could we send a couple pieces of cake to the valet crew? They're really sweet."

"Absolutely. Actually, the caterers are already boxing up food for the bridal party so I'll have them box up some more for them as well."

"For us?"

"Oh yeah! Hailey said her friends liked food and that we better send a bunch home with all of you."

"I love her so much," she said on a sigh, already missing her best friend while being simultaneously happy that Hailey was off on an adventure.

"Me too. I wish all my clients were like the two of them," she said almost wistfully. "They were a dream to work with and..." She cleared her throat, as if realizing who she was talking to.

"What?"

"Ah, just…I sort of expected Mr. Lennox to be uptight because of his money but he was one of the nicest people I've ever worked with. And their marriage is going to make it. I'm really good at predicting these things," she said on a smile that turned her from beautiful to out-of-this-world stunning.

Reese tried not to feel like a monster next to the woman. "Yeah they are."

"Jasmine!" One of the caterers called out and Jasmine gave Reese a dry smile.

"Duty calls. But I'll make sure to send out cake and snacks in a minute, promise. Oh, Cash was looking for you earlier. I think I saw him at the bar."

Reese made a noncommittal sound and headed out the open French doors into an outdoor patio and seating area. Even with the heat lamps there wasn't anyone here because the majority of people were at the reception.

Where Cash was supposedly waiting for her.

*Yeah, right.* Annoyed with herself for caring that he was currently banging someone else, she headed back to the reception, determined to dance and drink far too many glasses of champagne.

She smiled at a couple who passed her as she headed down the long walkway toward the middle of the maze, the music, laughter and voices growing louder.

"Hey, where'd you get off to?" Ezra strode up, tux jacket long discarded along with his bow tie. He held a beer in his big hand.

"Ah, just…nothing. What the hell is happening right now?" She stared at the dance floor where Roland, a former Ranger who worked for Jesse, and Bradford, one of their coworkers at Redemption Harbor Security, were… "Are they having a dance-off or something?"

"I believe there's a bet involved," Ezra murmured, laughter in his voice before he tipped his bottle back.

"I feel like I just stepped into an alternate reality," she murmured, turning toward the bar and stopping dead in her heels.

*Cash.*

He was at the bar, not screwing someone in his SUV. He was half turned in his seat, his jawline a gorgeous profile that a sculptor or painter would love, and watching the wild dance-off happening. When he saw her, he lifted a hand and half waved, that perpetual grin firmly in place.

As the strangest sense of relief rolled through her to see him, she made a beeline for him, ignoring when someone called out her name. "Hey, I thought I just saw you in the parking lot."

He blinked. "Ah, nope. Been here...looking for you. Where have you been anyway?"

"Oh, I had to take a phone call." Well, not technically true, but after she'd sent those pictures to her mom, she'd figured talking to her now was better than dealing with questions later. "You weren't just in your SUV?"

"I didn't even drive."

"You didn't?" Seriously, could the relief stop pummeling through her like a tsunami? Because this level of elation was beyond ridiculous.

He took a sip of what looked like water, shook his head. "Nope. Figured one of the guys would give me a ride home."

"Or...maybe I could give you a ride home." And a ride in her bed. Wait, had she said that out loud?

His green eyes darkened, his gaze sweeping over her in a rush of lust and hunger. "I'd love it if you'd give me a ride," he growled.

And oh, yeah, no mistaking his intent. Because there was no subtlety now.

"Want to get out of here?" she whispered.

Her words were barely out before he was off his stool and had taken her hand in his as he dragged her to the exit.

## Chapter 3

Reese stretched as she opened her eyes, then froze as she took in her surroundings. *Oooh.* Cash's bedroom. It wasn't like she'd exactly forgotten what they'd done last night.

And again this morning. Then another time. Wait, what time was it?

Bleary-eyed, she grabbed her cell from the nightstand, saw it was only seven. So she'd barely slept at all.

And where was Cash? Sitting up, she listened as she took in his bedroom in the daylight. When he'd moved to take the job with the Redemption Harbor Security branch in North Carolina, he'd bought a townhome downtown—though she knew he could have afforded a freaking mansion if he wanted. To be fair, he'd actually bought two townhomes, knocked down some walls to combine the two and now had a big-ass space.

Aaaaand she was getting all up in her head. She scrambled around, looking for her clothes, but only saw her panties. Her dress was nowhere to be seen and she was pretty sure they'd ripped it last night in their haste to get naked. That had been somewhere around the mudroom entrance from the garage.

Wanting to be dressed when she faced him, she stepped into his closet, found most of it was empty. And his closet was huge—much like the man himself. Ugh, she shelved that thought now, though it was hard considering she'd spent hours getting to intimately know exactly how large he was.

A few lonely, no doubt custom-made suits hung on one side. But it was mostly T-shirts, some expensive-looking sweaters and button-up shirts and a bunch of sneakers and boots. Okay, so he liked his footwear and spent more on that than his clothing, clearly.

She snagged a crisp white button-down shirt since it would cover her thighs, then went in search of him. There were no enticing scents of coffee or food, and she knew the man could cook. But the kitchen was empty, and when she checked the garage, it was empty.

*Huh.*

Heading back upstairs—and noticing the distinct lack of decorations or anything that screamed *this is Cash Pierce's place*—she dug around in one of his drawers and found a pair of sweatpants to wear. And that was when she saw the note from him, a quick scrawl in bold handwriting.

*Grabbing food, be back soon.*

And panic set in at those words as she made a split-second decision. She found her purse, double-checked that her keys were in it, couldn't find her dress so she just left it, and hurried to her car, which Cash had parked right out front. He'd been drinking water last night more than anything so he'd been fine to drive.

She told herself that she was doing them both a favor as she slid into the driver's seat and started her vehicle. That this would save them the awkward face-to-face conversation that was inevitable.

"Last night was fun, but we work together so this can't happen again." Ugh, she could practically hear his words. Or *worse*, he'd say something like, "Last night was fun, let's see where this goes." And then inevitably he'd cheat on her or decide that she wasn't good enough for him and be done. And she'd have her heart broken for the world to see and still have to work with him. Or quit, because she couldn't deal with working with him after having her heart broken.

*No thanks.*

Been there, done that, got the damn T-shirt.

She was saving them heartache, embarrassment, and awkwardness. Really, she was doing both of them a favor.

*Liar, liar*, the little voice in her head whispered. *You're just afraid to take a risk, to find out if someone can love you unconditionally.*

"Oh screw you," she growled to herself, then winced because she was talking to herself. Maybe that meant she'd officially lost it; she wasn't certain.

*Whatever.* She steered down his street, glad when she didn't pass him on the road because that would just add to the awkward. And right now she wanted to go home and wallow in her stupid decision-making skills.

And maybe replay how amazing last night had been, how many orgasms he'd wrung from her. Because that was super healthy. But there was no way she'd be forgetting that intense night with Cash.

No, she'd be obsessing about it for longer than she wanted to think about. And normally she'd call Hailey about something like this—not that she'd ever experienced anything like last night with anyone—but her girl was (a) on her honeymoon and (b) basically Cash's sister, so calling her was out of the question.

She'd just deal with this on her own—by burying her head in the sand.

***

Sighing, Cash tried to shove down his disappointment when he saw Reese's car missing from the curb.

"Knew I shouldn't have left," he muttered even as annoyance and something a lot deeper scored through him. Hailey had warned him that Reese was a runner, but he'd thought that after becoming friends, after the night they'd shared, that things were different between them.

Frustration growing by the time he parked and stepped into his place, he was surprised to find Reese's dress in his mudroom.

Because yeah, they'd started there. He'd gone down on her, then carried her to the kitchen where they'd had sex on his countertop. Then they'd made it to the stairs, done more there, then finally made it to his bedroom.

And he'd never brought a woman back to his place. Because this place was new and he'd only moved in a few months ago—but also even before Reese, he'd never brought anyone but serious girlfriends back to his place.

And he'd only had one serious relationship. Or what he thought was one, but had been a giant lie in the end.

So there was that.

He tossed the bag of pastries on the island countertop and sat, drinking his coffee. He looked at his phone, debating if he should call her and ask her what the hell, but texted Hailey instead.

And yeah, it was her honeymoon, but whatever. If she didn't want to respond, she wouldn't.

His phone rang moments later. "Hey, I didn't mean for you to call me." Now he actually felt like a dick.

"Oh, it's fine. Jesse is out getting us food," she said around a yawn. "We haven't left the room at all."

"TMI, sis." They might not be blood, but they were related in all the ways that mattered.

She just snickered, then said, "So, you ignored everything I said and hooked up with Reese?"

"Yeah. And I hate when you're right."

"I'm sorry, seriously. And for the record, I think she actually does like you."

"Actually?"

"You know what I mean. But she's a runner, has been for as long as I've known her. I think she got burned when she was in college and it messed with her head."

"You don't know for sure?"

"I mean, no, but even if I did, I don't think I'd tell you. I wouldn't want to violate her privacy. She's one of my best friends but she's always been pretty quiet about relationship stuff. Now, family stuff, not so much. Her parents set a very high standard and she feels like she'll never meet their expectations."

"I guess that's the good part about being a foster kid," he muttered, even though it was a lie. He'd have killed for stability, a family growing up. Something he'd only experienced once he'd met Hailey, Jesse and Easton.

"Yeah, maybe." There was a hesitant note in her voice.

"What?"

"Nothing. I don't want to like, give bad advice or anything, but…I hope you don't give up on her."

"I'm not giving up on anything." Or anyone.

She sighed and he could practically hear the smile in her voice. "Good. I think you two complement each other in a way I didn't see at first. She needs a sunshine Cash in her life."

"I'm not sunshine."

"Well…you're not grumpy, and I think I'm only saying this because I'm dealing with jet lag and had too many mimosas on the plane, but you're kind of wonderful, you big dumbass."

"I'm a dumbass now?"

"You're also *wonderful* and exactly what she needs. And I think she's what you need. Oh, Jesse's back and he's got food so I've gotta go. But I love you and call if you need anything."

"I'll text and don't worry about me. Enjoy the hell out of your honeymoon. Love both of you guys."

After she disconnected, he set his phone on his countertop and leaned back. He hadn't been lying to Hailey either. He wasn't giving up.

Not on Reese. Because he didn't want something casual, and after being with her, he knew he couldn't settle for anything else.

But he couldn't run straight at her. No, not with her being a runner. He had to deal with this carefully, because this wasn't a game and he wasn't going to lose.

## Chapter 4

*Two days later*

"Just act normal. Everything is fine. I'm fine. Totally fine," Reese murmured to herself as she parked in the secure lot of Redemption Harbor Security. Next to Cash's Land Rover. So he was definitely here. Which was great. *Totally* great.

Skye had taken over their North Carolina branch while Hailey was on her honeymoon, and Reese had woken up to a text simply saying, *Hey, can you come in to the office when you're up?*

So it was now nine and Reese's stomach was all twisted in knots because she had no clue what this was about.

And she'd been too scared to ask. What if this was about her and Cash? They were coworkers, and while there wasn't, like, anything specific in the employee handbook about dating—the two founders were married and she knew others had met while working—maybe she'd screwed up somehow?

*Get it together!* she silently ordered herself as she stepped out onto the concrete of the enclosed parking lot next to Redemption Harbor Security's warehouse. This was their real place of business, not the front they had downtown with the cute little office nestled between a lawyer's office and a professional decorator's office.

After having her face and palm scanned, Reese stepped inside and made her way to the conference room Skye had indicated.

As she stepped inside, she saw that it wasn't just Skye and Cash, but Rowan and a redhead she recognized from Hailey's pictures. Adalyn. "Hey, am I late?" She sat at the conference table—two chairs behind Cash, hoping it didn't look obvious that she was trying to keep her distance. She sure hadn't cared about distance two days ago.

"No, you're on time," Skye said with an easy smile. Her long auburn hair was pulled back into a loose ponytail, the style a little different than her usual tight braid. Even with it being winter, her light olive skin was a few shades darker than normal, maybe from the last job she'd been on. Even though she was an average height for a woman, something about Skye seemed bigger than life, always had. Maybe it was her beauty, ice-blue eyes and confidence—or maybe it was the fact that she was a former spy with mad skills who'd once single-handedly destroyed a Mexican cartel's compound while rescuing a doctor in the middle of the night in enemy territory. Probably the second thing.

A little bark alerted her that Skye had brought her dog C-4 as well as Hailey and Jesse's new dog, a corgi named Pumpkin. He was curled up on a dog bed next to Skye, and C-4 was lying directly on top of their dog as if he was her pillow. He let out another yip, and moved his legs as if he was dreaming about running.

"We've had a job pop up and it's perfect for the four of you. Adalyn, this is Reese. You guys can get to know each other later but I want to run down what the deal is first."

Cash glanced over his shoulder at Reese and gave her a warm smile.

Which just threw her for a loop. After banging his brains out Saturday night, she'd run from his place like a coward. It had seemed like a good idea at the time, but even on the mad dash home she'd had regrets. So many of them. Then she'd ignored his calls and texts because... *Regrets*.

She smiled back but it felt strained, as if she couldn't get her face muscles to work properly.

"To cut to the chase," Skye continued, "someone has potentially gone missing from Kingston Wellness Resort in Montana. It's an exclusive place where couples go to get away. Some who need to reconnect, and some who are just looking for a nice vacation. It's touted as being cut off from civilization. And while it sort of is, the amenities are all five-star, and there's Wi-Fi. It's just in a very remote place. And it definitely has a specific type of clientele."

Skye focused on Cash now. "Cash, because of who you are, you're going to be using your real name. And so are you, Reese. You two are going in as a recently engaged couple. Rowan, Adalyn, you two will also be going undercover as well, but you'll actually be using fake identities."

Reese glanced at the other two and could practically feel the tension vibrating between them. It might as well have been a live thing in the air. Rowan was normally laid-back and almost jovial, but right now the big man was tense, all the muscles in his forearms tight across his chest as he sat there, practically stewing. These two definitely did not like each other. She frowned, wondering what the deal was.

"You have a question, Reese?" Skye asked.

She wanted to ask Skye if she was sure about putting these two together but figured the woman had more info than she did. So she smiled and shook her head. "Nope, I'm good."

"Excellent. I've got packets for all of you going over all the pertinent information, but to give you a quick rundown, an employee who works there, one of their massage therapists, reached out and said a guide disappeared about a week ago. The owners said that she quit and returned home but this employee said she saw someone sneak into her friend's cabin in the middle of the night and leave with a bag of her stuff. The missing one, Aubry, isn't on great terms with her family but her mother is concerned, said that if Aubry had quit, she likely would have at least contacted her for a place to crash. We're still doing research," Skye said looking at Reese.

"I've got Gage running that side for this op because I want you on the ground. I think you and Cash will make a great team. I also think this will be a good opportunity to see how the two of you work together and how he does in action."

Cash nodded, and even though Reese could only see the back of his head she figured he was probably smiling. "I'm ready to get out there."

"Like I said, you all have a week to prepare." She looked at all four of them as she continued. "It's all in the files. I wish we could get you in earlier, but that wasn't possible. Also, you won't be flying in on a private jet, but commercial."

"You don't have a private jet?" Reese asked Cash before she could think about censoring herself.

He glanced back at her and shook his head.

She knew Jesse did, and she'd assumed Cash did as well. For some reason she was glad he didn't have one.

Skye handed out physical packets to all of them which felt old-school to Reese but she started flipping through the papers anyway. She would read everything later on her laptop but wanted to get familiar with who they were looking for and what the game plan was.

"You're sure there's no way we can get on the ground sooner?" she asked as she scanned the first page. It was a brief outline of the two owners—Mila and Ben Kingston. From their photos, they were both attractive, fit, and relatively tall. They both looked like they'd be comfortable wrangling cattle, riding horses and climbing mountains.

"We could fly you in earlier, but we can't get you into the wellness center before next Sunday. They have really strict time frames for when they do pickups and checkouts. It's always on a Sunday. The town next to it is too small for you guys to show up early and blend. You would be noticed, and from the intel we have, the missing employee rarely ventured into town anyway. She spent almost all of her time at the ranch. We're currently doing a deep dive on every employee who works there, but that's something you can help out with this week as well," Skye said as she looked at Reese.

Reese nodded and looked back down at the next page, this one going over the missing employee. Aubry Boyle. A pretty brunette with a wide smile was looking out at the camera, her dark eyes warm.

And Reese had a really bad feeling about her. She just hoped she was wrong.

# Chapter 5

Rowan remained seated where he was, waiting as the other three filed out, Adalyn shooting him a dark look before she stalked out behind Reese and Cash.

He pretended to ignore her, which was basically impossible. And he hated how gorgeous she was. It just…pissed him off even more about everything. She was just walking around, living her life, while his team was dead. He wasn't sure how the hell he was going to pretend to be a couple with the traitorous woman.

"So what's up?" Skye asked the moment the door shut behind the others. As she spoke, she leaned down and scooped up her little mutt who made purring sounds. The tiny ball of fluff was basically masquerading as a dog.

"Why are you pairing me with Adalyn? You could have paired her up with anyone else. Or me, for that matter. And why the hell did you hire her?" Okay well, now he was shouting. *Balls.* He'd meant to remain calm and professional, not shout at his boss—and friend. A woman he respected more than almost anyone.

"Are you questioning my ability to run this company?" Skye's tone was dry, her eyes flinty. Her auburn hair was pulled away from her face. Unlike Adalyn, who had rich, bright red hair that looked like flames, Skye's was a bit darker.

And why was he comparing the two? He didn't care what Adalyn looked like or how shiny or beautiful her hair was. "No. But I am questioning your decision to hire her. You know her backstory, right?"

"I do," she said in the same dry tone. "I'm just not sure you do."

He blinked. "What the hell does that mean?"

"It means..." Skye took a deep breath, then pushed it out as if she was practicing patience. Something she was shockingly good at, even if she liked to claim otherwise. "Look, I think she's right for this job. And if you guys can work together and act professional, it will show me what I need to know about you."

Aaaand he blinked again. "What does that mean?"

"I need someone who can run this place anytime Hailey is gone. Reese could easily handle it. So could Elijah, for that matter, but neither of them want to be in charge. They love what they do, and at the end of the day, I need someone who's a leader the way she is. I'm trying to figure out who would be the best to fill in for her. I'd hoped it was you but if you can't manage to make nice with another professional, then maybe my judgment is wrong."

He gritted his teeth. Skye wasn't in the habit of testing them so this surprised him, but maybe it shouldn't. They all worked together for a common cause, and yeah, he wouldn't mind calling the shots. Hell, he wouldn't mind running his own branch one day if they expanded. They were making a big difference in the world, helping people who had no one else to turn to. He blew out a breath as he spoke aloud the thing he normally kept buried deep, pain he masked with an easy smile. "She got my guys killed. She didn't press the detonator on that bomb, but she might as well have."

Skye opened her mouth, then snapped it shut. Then she opened it again. "Can you work with her or not?" she finally asked, surprising him.

He was under the impression that she was holding something back from him and it simultaneously pissed him off and made him curious. Was he missing something? Skye had impeccable judgment, something he couldn't say about the majority of people he knew. Himself included. Because he'd made a lot of mistakes in life. But Skye had a knack for looking at the bigger picture so he was going to trust her. "I can work with her."

"Good. And you have to be *convincing*," she added. "This job isn't about you or her or anyone's ego. It's about a missing woman. We need to find her."

Gathering up the file she'd given him, he nodded. "You can count on me."

He hoped.

# CHAPTER 6

Reese smiled politely at Adalyn Bonnevie, their newest employee—apparently. She knew Hailey had been friends with the woman. Cash too, clearly, considering the way he was joking around with her as they stepped into the parking lot.

"So when did Skye hire you?" Cash asked as they approached their row of vehicles.

Adalyn's Jeep was on the other side of Cash's SUV and of course she had a cool vehicle—a bright purple Jeep was just plain fun. Little ducks lined the front of the dash and there was a peace sticker on the back.

"Ah, she's been trying to hire me for years. Finally said yes." Her voice was throaty, some might say sexy, and her tone was dry. But there was a bit of humor in it too as she looked at Cash. "She's hard to say no to."

"True enough," Reese murmured.

Adalyn smiled at her. "Hailey messaged me about you before the wedding, said she was glad we were finally getting to meet. I got there late or we'd have likely met then."

Reese grinned at her. "Well if Hailey likes you, then I know I will. If you want to get together sometime this week before the op, let me know. We can do drinks, dinner, whatever."

Adalyn blinked, looking faintly surprised, but then nodded. "That'd be great, thanks."

"Uh, am I invited to this?" Cash asked.

"Of course." Because she was a professional. Mostly. Probably. She could hang out with a coworker/friend after having a couple hours of hot, sweaty sex. Easy peasy. It had been one time, no big deal. Except, his dick was a very big deal. *Gah!* Why couldn't her brain just shut up? "We'll set something up."

"Great." Adalyn smiled as she shoved her hands in her jeans pockets. "Cash has my number so you can just grab it from him. I'm going to start memorizing everything but I'm open all week."

"Sounds good." Reese slid her sunglasses on as Adalyn headed for her Jeep, needing a small barrier from Cash now that it was just the two of them. "So what's up with her and Rowan?" she whispered, even though Adalyn was already pulling out of the parking lot.

Cash paused, looked conflicted, but then gave her an easy smile. "Honestly, I don't know. But he'll deal, he's a professional." He cleared his throat, looking more gorgeous than any man had a right to. Tall, with dark hair, a killer jawline, and forearms and biceps she dreamed about—especially after experiencing first-hand how flexible and capable he was in the bedroom. "I was thinking, if we're supposed to be engaged, then you'll need a ring."

"Oh, right. We've got a bunch of props and other things for undercover jobs. I'm sure there are some flashy engagement rings in the stash."

He shook his head and pressed the key fob on his vehicle. "Nah, we're going to do this right. I already called a local jewelry store. We're going to sell this, and it'll leave a real trail if someone decides to look deeper into us. Which I kind of doubt, but it's good to have our bases covered. Skye knows we're doing this," he added.

*Oh.* "Ah, okay. I can just meet you there?"

"If you want. Or I can just drive us so we look like a happily engaged couple when we show up together."

She narrowed her gaze at him from behind her sunglasses, unable to tell if he was messing with her. Well if he was, she wasn't going to let it bother her. "Okay, let's go."

When she was sitting in the comfy, warm interior of his SUV, she turned on the seat warmer.

"How do you already have a jeweler since you just moved here a couple months ago?" Was he buying jewelry for other women? The thought had her frowning again.

Cash had moved to North Carolina after selling his billion-dollar construction empire not too long ago. According to Hailey, he'd been floundering, trying to figure out what he wanted to do with his life. Because also according to Hailey, Cash got bored quickly and often moved on—which told her a lot about him. The reason he was nicknamed Cash was because everything he touched seemed to make money. Even when he'd been in the army, he'd done some shady business running vodka on base. The real reason he'd originally made it big was because he'd invested in a handful of things—mainly apps created by Jesse Lennox—when he'd been just eighteen. And those investments had paid off big. Since then it was like big piles of cash just fell into his lap on the regular.

"Technically they're not 'my' jeweler. I just asked Jesse to hook me up and he gave us a solid recommendation."

That made sense. "Have you talked to either of them since they left?"

"Yeah, I've texted with them a bit, but they're obviously busy."

Reese snickered. "Yeah, I've gotten a few pictures from Hailey but I'm trying not to bother her too much. They deserve this time together."

"Yeah they do."

Reese loved how close Cash was with both Hailey and Jesse—and loved watching the banter between the three of them. Well four, when Easton, their other former foster brother, was around. Hailey and Cash acted like straight-up kids sometimes and it was refreshing to see her best friend let loose and relax. She was always so serious with work, which made sense, but Hailey needed to have fun in her life. And Cash brought out that side of her.

"So..." Cash cleared his throat.

Oh god, here it came. He was going to bring up what happened Saturday night. Not just ignore it like she desperately wanted him to. She knew she shouldn't have gotten in the damn vehicle.

"I was thinking that maybe we should ask Adalyn if she wants to do breakfast tomorrow. Maybe that diner downtown, the one you like? We could also ask Rowan, but maybe not for the first meetup."

Reese felt oddly disappointed that he hadn't brought up the night of the wedding, but then chastised herself. Still, it was annoying that he was acting like nothing happened when not too long ago he'd had his face buried between her legs as he'd made her come.

*So. Many. Times.*

Jeez, the amount of orgasms he'd wrung out of her... She turned off the seat heater because she was already warm enough.

"That's a great idea," she managed to rasp out. Just freaking great.

\*\*\*

Cash glanced down at Reese as Naima Friedman the owner of the boutique jewelry store showed them to a back room clearly reserved for appointments. They wouldn't be open for another hour, but Cash knew the woman had come in specifically for him. At least his money was good for something.

"Can I interest the two of you in anything to drink? Coffee, cappuccino, mimosas..."

"Ah, sparkling water for me," Reese said with a smile.

"Coffee for me."

"A bit of cream and sugar on the side for him," Reese added as she reached out and squeezed his hand with hers.

Aaaand he loved when she touched him, even briefly. Especially after Saturday night—and technically Sunday morning. She'd kissed him, caressed him everywhere, had completely let loose and been just as wild and free in bed as he'd hoped she'd be. Hell, better than he'd fantasized.

Before she'd run out like a damn coward.

That was okay, however. He wasn't giving up. Nope, he was simply re-strategizing where she was concerned. Which meant he couldn't ask a bunch of questions about why she'd left after the most intense night of his life. Nope. He couldn't make things awkward or give her a reason to run again.

He was going to do exactly what she was doing—act normal. Though he'd seen the covert looks she kept shooting him. She wasn't as unaffected as she'd like him to believe.

"Thanks, babe," he murmured, wrapping his arm around her and pulling her close to him as they sat on the cushy love seat.

The private room had a few tables already set up with glittering rings on display in velvet-lined boxes. The kind that would never be for sale in the front of the store. This place was already high-end with exclusive clients, per Jesse. But given their location in the historic downtown, he guessed they saw a lot of foot traffic. Especially since there were two small restaurants on either side of the place, both which had well-publicized happy hours and Sunday brunches with cheap mimosas.

Yeah, he could just see people strolling by here and making impulse purchases to the tune of a few hundred bucks. Hmm, maybe he should see about investing or opening something downtown? There were a few spaces he'd seen for sale near the edge of the main street.

"Your rings are beautiful," Reese said, pulling him out of his thoughts as Naima set their drinks on a gold tray on the table in front of them.

"Thank you. I take pride in selecting all the gems myself. Now, I hear that the two of you are looking for an engagement ring and wedding set so tell me exactly what you're looking for."

"Oh...any one of those is beautiful." Reese nodded at the table closest to them.

But Cash ignored the rings. "None of these are right for my soon to be *wife*." Damn, he really did like the way that sounded, and knew it should terrify him. "She works with her hands a lot and doesn't want something that will catch on her clothing. And she doesn't like anything flashy. She hates diamonds so those are out too. If there are any gems, they need to be embedded in the metal. Since her favorite color is green, I think specifically green sapphires would work well." He looked down at her. "What do you think?"

Reese blinked up at him, looking dazed.

Yeah, that was good. He needed to keep this complicated woman on her toes, get a ring on her finger. Then before she realized it, he'd have her locked down forever. Because this woman was it for him, even if she was still running. He knew it at the most primal level, even if he wanted to deny it. Even if he'd never thought marriage would be for him. He just hadn't met the right person.

"I respect a man who understands his partner," Naima said quietly, a smile in her voice as she looked between the two of them.

Reese cleared her throat, then looked back at the other woman. "Everything he said is correct."

"I can come up with some sketches, then we'll narrow down exactly what you want. From there, I'll create an image with a custom program I use, but this kind of order will take time."

"That's no issue," Cash said smoothly. "I would like to have a placeholder ring for her, just for the near future. We're taking a trip and I want everyone to know she's all mine."

Naima beamed at him and nodded in approval.

"I'll also want to look at earrings and a few other things today as well."

Reese nudged him, but he ignored her. Because he was buying her jewelry and staking a claim.

An hour later, she had a ring on her left-hand ring finger—a simple gold band with nine small green sapphires. Fine for now. He'd also bought her earrings and a couple bracelets, much to her annoyance.

But he didn't care.

"Thank you again," he murmured to Naima as she walked them out. "I'll be in touch later."

She nodded, smiling widely at both of them as they stepped out onto the sidewalk. "I look forward to it, Mr. Pierce."

"Constantine, please."

She nodded and shut the door behind her, the little bell jingling as it moved.

"What the heck was that?" Reese kept her smile firmly in place, but it was fake as hell as she slid her sunglasses back on. As she did, the gold bracelet he'd bought for her glinted under the sunlight.

It was a simple enough bangle, a knot cuff bracelet that shouldn't get in her way. The earrings were... Well, fine, they were over-the-top emerald earrings but whatever. They looked good on her, and all he could think about was her wearing just them while she rode him, the gems flashing in the sunlight as she cried out his name.

He adjusted her scarf and leaned down slightly, enjoying her intake of breath as he gently kissed her cheek. "I take care of my woman," he murmured against her ear. "It won't look right if we show up for this undercover gig and I haven't put my mark on you."

She sucked in another breath, then pushed at his chest. "Put your mark on me?" she snapped, all that fire he loved sparking in her eyes.

He grinned. "I wondered if that would piss you off," he murmured, stepping back but not putting any distance between them. "I'm just messing with you. But this is important for me, to get this job right. We need to play the part perfectly and find Aubry Boyle."

Her expression softened and she linked her arm in his. "Yeah, you're right. But I'm not, like, *keeping* any of this after the job. You can return it or give it away or...whatever."

Cash simply grunted, not giving a response one way or another. Because he sure as hell wasn't taking it back. And he'd lied; he hadn't run anything by Skye. He'd simply wanted to buy something for Reese.

# Chapter 7

*Five days later*

Cash was out of the back of the hired vehicle before Reese could think about opening her door and had pulled their bags from the back of the SUV.

She hadn't seen him since they'd gone jewelry shopping days ago despite plans to meet up with Adalyn. That, she'd actually done. They'd had breakfast a couple times and gotten to know each other—though Reese felt like she was barely skimming the surface of actually knowing the other woman. Cash had been absent, however.

So when a driver had picked her up this morning, she'd been far too excited to see Cash.

As she stepped onto the curb, he had their two suitcases pushed together and was thanking their driver as she stood guard by the bags—and tried not to look at her fake engagement ring again.

She hadn't worn it in the last week, but she'd slipped it on early this morning while finishing packing up and...wasn't sure how she felt about it. Weird, mostly.

Because she hated that she actually liked the way the ring looked. He'd been right. She would have hated something flashy, and this ring was simple and wouldn't catch on anything. She wondered if he'd remembered to cancel his custom order, hoped he had so he wouldn't be out all that money.

As she watched him smile at the driver, she found herself annoyed with Cash for reasons that made no sense. She was the one who'd run from him, and he'd been perfectly professional all week: texting her to check in about their op and then last night to let her know he'd hired a driver to pick them both up.

So now here they were and he was just taking over everything—which was really nice, if she was being honest. Sure, it was part of their cover, but she could admit that she liked this side of him.

A little. Or a lot. Whatever. It was probably just part of his cover too, being the caring, thoughtful fiancé.

By the time they were checked in, their bags checked, they headed to the Executive Level lounge and found two dark blue recliners that faced the nearby runway. In the last few years she'd mostly flown on the company jet because of the nature of their work, but everything about this job was different.

And she couldn't stop the worry for the missing woman, especially since over the last week she and Gage—one of the founders who was located in the South Carolina flagship office—hadn't found anything from Aubry on social media or any movements on her credit or debit cards. For the most part, she'd been pretty sparse about using her debit card anyway, but the woman had posted almost daily on social media. Usually pictures of nature, hiking trails, canoeing, or kayaking trips, and now there was a distinct lack of anything from her. Unfortunately the lack of posts was telling.

"Are you hungry or thirsty?" Cash stretched out on the chair next to hers, but didn't put the footrest up.

"Ah, I'm good, you don't have to get me anything."

"I'll get anything for my future wife."

Oh, he was really laying this on thick even though it was just the two of them. Despite the weird sensation in her stomach, she laughed. "Okay, future husband, cappuccino is actually good. I didn't make anything this morning." Because she'd overslept, then run around like a wild chicken trying to make sure she hadn't forgotten anything. That was why she liked the back-end side of ops—when she was doing straight analysis and hacking, she didn't have to worry about interacting with people, or wearing clothes other than jeans and oversized sweaters.

His forest green eyes went all smoky when she said *husband* and oh...oh, she could feel that heat twining through her, curling out to all her nerve endings. "No problem," he murmured, then frowned at his phone as he stood. He tossed it to her. "Will you please assure Hailey that we're fine without her? She's sent me eighteen texts this morning alone, fluctuating between encouraging me and calling me a dumbass."

Reese snickered as she caught the phone, which was already open for her to use. Aaand oh sweet pandas, he was *serious*.

She texted back, *Hailey! This is Reese, your boy is fine! I'm fine. Everything is fine. Now how's the honeymoon? Have you had your brains banged out yet?*

There was a long pause, then three little dots popped up, then... A bunch of eggplants and peaches appeared.

*Something is seriously wrong with you. Also, I can see you cackling right now.*

*Haaa, you know me so well! Honeymoon is great, I'm just worried and it's weird not working...and weird not being there for Cash's first job.*

*It's all good. I promise.* Reese knew how much Hailey loved the other man, understood now how much Hailey had been keeping from Reese about her past. *I'll keep him safe!*

*How about you both keep each other safe? Also, I bought you a bunch of chocolate at this little place in Paris and you're going to love it.*

*Aww, thanks. I'm sure I will. I also love you! Now go enjoy your honeymoon and stop worrying about us. Cash is trained and professional. We've got this.*

*Impossible not to worry, but fine, Jesse is getting annoyed now anyway.* Aaand that was followed by more eggplant emojis.

Reese snorted out a laugh and had started to tuck his phone away when another text popped up.

*Darling, I miss you and was hoping we could talk...*

Reese blinked once, twice, then closed the phone. Because she wasn't going to open up the full message. Nope, that was a can of worms that wasn't her business.

Even if she found herself very, very annoyed that Isabella Vance, Cash's ex, was texting him.

"So I got you egg bites and some fruit since I figured you didn't eat either."

Blinking out of her haze, she smiled up at Cash. "Thanks, that's really sweet. I think I've also gotten Hailey off your case. She's just worried about you, that's all. I think not seeing you guys for so long, then being separated from you and Easton, especially after Easton got kidnapped, is just weighing on her."

He gave a soft smile. "Yeah, she's always had a big heart."

"She also texted a bunch of peach and eggplant emojis so fair warning."

He snort-laughed and almost dropped his own coffee as he sat down next to her, propped his feet up. "Those two were always like rabbits, I swear," he said, shaking his head as she handed his phone back to him.

He didn't open it or look at his phone so...should she tell him about the text? Nope, he'd just see it later and she didn't want to dig deeper into his personal life. Reese had once asked him about Isabella the night she'd met the other woman—they'd also been sort of undercover that night as well. Cash very much hadn't wanted to talk about her, so she would respect his privacy.

And bury her curiosity.

For now anyway. Okay, not at all, because was he in contact with his ex? Or was this something new... *Ugh*. She had to stop getting up in her head about this.

Right now she needed to focus on their job.

*The. Job.*

"Adalyn's at the airport," she murmured as she looked at her own phone, saw the incoming text. "Rowan too. They're going to avoid this lounge," she murmured, looking over her shoulder.

There weren't that many people here this early, but the ones who were had already attacked the breakfast buffet and she couldn't blame them. Her coffee was amazing and she assumed everything else was just as good.

Cash nodded as he leaned back in his chair. "I just wish we were there already, I hate all this waiting around."

Yeah, she did too.

As she took another sip of her coffee, her phone buzzed with another text, this one from Gage, hacker extraordinaire. And what she read made her stomach drop.

"Look at this," she murmured, glancing around again before holding out her phone to Cash.

He frowned at her phone. "What is this?"

"A picture 'Aubry' posted an hour ago of a hiking trail she likes. Gage says the metadata has been deleted or it just isn't available, but there's no snow on the ground. He's running the image to see if he can figure out more about it, but it's similar to some others she's posted."

"And it's currently snowing where we're going," he murmured, his frown growing at the lack of snow in the picture. The image was of a hiking trail with bare trees on either side, green, yellow and brown leaves scattered in front of the viewer like a blanket. Stunning, sure, but it was way too cold in Montana right now for this to be recent.

His frown mirrored her own as she sat back in the lounge chair, worry for the missing woman growing by the second.

# Chapter 8

"So I'm Cash and this is Reese," Cash said to the others in the van that had picked them up from the airport. The shuttle was exclusive to the wellness center/resort and was transporting them as well as two other couples. "We're here to relax before we start planning our wedding." He held up Reese's left hand to be a bit obnoxious as he showed off the faux engagement ring and was rewarded when she gave him a dry look. But he loved the way her mouth curved up slightly at the edges. He loved her smiles, her almost-smiles and...even when she was glaring daggers at him.

"Ah, I'm Rick," Rowan said, leaning into his undercover persona. "And this is my wife, Ava."

Adalyn smiled at them and then turned to smile at the couple in the third row of the van.

"I'm Bode," the man from the back said, his smile a bit tight. "And this is my wife, Rae."

The pretty blonde smiled at them, but hers was tight as well. She looked like she wanted to be anywhere but where they were, so maybe this was a last-ditch effort on their marriage.

Cash turned back around when it was clear that this wasn't a chatty group and wrapped his arm around Reese, who leaned into him.

She had her phone out and texted him. *Looks like a couple more pictures popped up on Aubry's IG account, this time with the quote 'Fun memories.' Maybe whoever is posting is trying to cover up for their last post.*

*Or maybe it's really her?* he texted back, but added a frowny face emoji, because neither of them believed that.

*No, Gage said that the phone turned on, posted, then turned off almost immediately. And it pinged off a cell tower nearby the wellness center. He couldn't pinpoint where it was coming from exactly, but Aubry's cell phone never left Montana.*

Which meant she likely hadn't either—she'd allegedly told the owners that she was moving back home to the East Coast. Cash's stomach tightened as he accepted that if someone had the woman's phone and was fake posting, then the chances of her being truly gone were a lot higher. *Do we involve anyone else?* he texted, meaning law enforcement. He figured the answer was no, but he was new to the team.

*Definitely too soon to do that. Her friend already tried and was shot down multiple times by the local sheriff's department. When we get there, we'll talk to the friend who reported her missing and go from there.*

Instead of texting, he simply kissed the top of her head and looked out the window at the snowcapped mountains in the distance. Snow covered the land in either direction as they cruised down the two-lane highway, with thick fir trees sprouting up among the blanket of white. There was a ski slope not too far from the wellness center, but the owners of this place wanted the focus to be more on partners reconnecting through things like hiking, yoga, meditation, horseback riding, couples' massages. And there were multiple classes, including wellness ones and one on tantric sex. Which...sounded interesting. Or it would, under different circumstances.

"We're here," said their driver, a burly-looking man in his sixties who'd grunted about four words the entire drive. "Careful when you get out. I've got the bags and they'll be delivered to your individual cabins."

And that was that. Cash shoved the door open, was hit with a blast of cold as his boots crunched on the thin layer of slushy snow. When Reese went to get out, he lifted her up and over the slushy part and set her on the cleared part of the path—and got a smile of thanks.

Before they'd taken a couple steps toward what was a designated walking path that connected about a dozen or more cabins, three people wearing thick purple jackets, purple snow-proof pants appeared, each carrying two glasses of champagne.

"I'm Joelle." The woman in front of them handed them each a glass and smiled politely at both of them. "I'll show you to your cabin and go over everything before the meet and greet in an hour. Your bags will be delivered shortly and you'll have enough time to freshen up before meeting with the owners."

The others were getting a similar speech from employees so Cash fell in step with Reese, politely taking a sip of the champagne, but nothing more than that. He wanted a clear head for this job.

The walk to their cabin didn't take long, thankfully, but he found himself impatient, wanting to jump right into things. Reese had warned him that he'd have to be patient and he knew she was right. Didn't mean he had to like it.

"This place is gorgeous," Reese murmured as they reached the steps that led up to a huge patio attached to the stone and wood cabin.

The cabin was almost an A-frame, with slightly slanted roofs to keep the snow off, but slightly wide—more chalet in style than anything. The entire back of the cabin was windows, including the upstairs and downstairs, revealing the cozy-looking interior. A spacious living room and fireplace was on the left side while the kitchen was on the right. A stone fireplace dominated the middle of the house, with the fireplace clearly providing heat to the interior and even the exterior patio. He could partially see upstairs, but from his angle couldn't get a good enough view. Had to be the bedroom though.

"The hot tub has already been turned on and is perfect if you'd like to try it out," Joelle said, motioning to the six-seater on the corner of the patio.

There was no snow anywhere on the back seating area so clearly they had people coming in to keep things up for their guests.

Cash simply nodded politely, as did Reese, as the woman unlocked the back door and ushered them inside. She continued telling them about the place, the amenities, and who they could call if they needed anything. Then she paused, lowered her voice.

"You're Cash and Reese? You're here to help, right?" she murmured, her dark eyes intent with worry.

"We are," Reese said, her expression warm. "You're the one who reached out about your friend?"

The woman, who Cash only realized now had to be in her early twenties, looked young and vulnerable as she stared between the two of them. "I am. I can't talk now because we're on a schedule, but I'll be back after the meet and greet. I'll add that you requested extra towels and champagne and bring everything then."

"That sounds good," Reese said. "Do you feel safe right now? If not, let us know and we'll get you out of here immediately."

The blonde blinked, but then half-smiled. "I'm fine. I think..." She glanced out the bank of windows into the darkening evening, then back at them. "I didn't say anything when I reached out but I think Aubry was sleeping with someone who works here."

Reese's eyes widened slightly, but she kept her smile firmly in place and Cash just followed her lead. "That's good to know, thank you. Do you know who she was seeing?"

"Well..." Joelle bit her bottom lip. "No. I don't know for sure and I'd just be speculating."

"If your friend is missing, we need all the information to help us paint a better picture of where she might be. We're not here to judge anyone and we simply want to find your friend."

Joelle shoved out a breath and nodded. "Okay. Yeah, I know I should have said something but I didn't know if... I thought maybe you wouldn't take this job if you thought she..." She cleared her throat, seemed to steel herself. "I'm pretty sure she was sleeping with Mr. Kingston."

The married owner of the Kingston Wellness Resort.

## Chapter 9

Rowan glanced around the interior of the cabin, surprised by how huge it was. Had to be right at twenty-five hundred square feet. These were full-on homes, not vacation chalets like he'd imagined.

The person who'd shown them to the cabin had given them a detailed spiel about what to expect, then left quietly.

Adalyn stepped back into the kitchen, looking annoyingly gorgeous. But her expression was neutral, nothing like back when he'd known her. Back when they'd been friends. Before everything had gone to shit. She had a little brochure in her hand and didn't look up as she said, "We can figure out sleeping arrangements later but we need to at least pretend to be sharing a bed. We can make up the guest bed or whatever every morning."

"I don't need you to tell me how to do my job," he snapped way more forcefully than he'd meant to.

She looked up in surprise, with a touch of injury in her dark eyes, aaaand he felt like an asshole. He shoved down that feeling even as her neutral mask fell back in place.

"I wasn't trying to tell you what to do," she said on a sigh.

*Damn it.* He knew how much sexism she'd dealt with at the CIA and he realized he sounded like just another asshole. Probably because he was one. But not because of sexism. He scrubbed a hand over his face even as he told himself to apologize.

"Maybe tomorrow we can plan a hike and use the time to break into one of the employees' cabins or even the owners'. Or maybe we can try searching the surrounding area," she murmured more to herself. "There are just too many places to hide a body around here, unfortunately."

Yeah, he'd thought the same thing when they'd arrived. So much wide-open space and territory mostly untouched by humans. And plenty of animals to finish the job if someone dumped a body. He grunted in response because he was pissed at her and pissed at himself—and this entire situation. He didn't want to be working undercover with her. Didn't want to be in the same state as her.

But Skye was right. If he wanted to run the team, he needed to get his shit together. He'd never had a problem running his own team in the Marines. But then he'd—

"Jesus, I'm going to grab some hot cocoa at the meeting place. You can just join me there," she growled, pulling him out of his thoughts.

"What?"

She glared at him as she tossed the pamphlet on the countertop, a hint of the Adalyn he remembered there. "I get that you hate me, you sanctimonious prick. But we're on a job, and while I've dealt with bigger assholes than you, I actually expected you to be professional. So let's make a deal—we'll fake it in public, and in private we'll only talk about the job. But that means you have to actually respond when I talk. Because I won't work with you otherwise. And it's not like I'm going to be working in your branch anyway. Skye thought my skill set would be good for this job, but I'm going to be out of the other office. So if you can pull your head out of your ass for a while, let's find this missing woman even if she's dead so we can give her mother some goddamn peace." Her hands were balled into fists as she stalked past him, but by the time she got to one of the back doors, her body language had softened and he knew her expression would be calm and neutral as she stepped out into the world.

Because she'd always been a pro. Back when she'd been embedded with them in Afghanistan, he'd watched her charm everyone around her.

Including him.

He picked up the brochure, then grabbed his suitcase—an expensive one that was part of his cover, because normally he just traveled with a duffel bag—and stalked upstairs.

As he'd expected, Adalyn had set her suitcase neatly by the closet and put her toiletry bag on the countertop in the bathroom. No perfumes out, no fuss, no muss. Just like the woman he remembered.

Once he'd cleaned up and changed into new clothes, he headed out to find his partner.

He ordered himself to keep it together, to be a total professional from this point forward and apologize.

He was the king at compartmentalizing, he could certainly do it for however long they were in Montana.

The snow-dusted path right outside their cabin was lit up with little solar lights every foot, creating a magical setting. Everything about this place was incredible, the sky so clear and vast it reminded him of home.

He found Adalyn, aka Ava, sitting with the woman who had been on the bus with them that afternoon.

They both had thick, insulated mugs of what he guessed was hot cocoa, considering the servers walking around with little jars of marshmallows and other toppings. This place was definitely over-the-top but it was clear they provided what they advertised—a place to relax and reconnect with your loved one.

He'd certainly slept in a hell of a lot worse places. So had Adalyn, for that matter. And he hated that they weren't friends anymore, that they couldn't joke around, but there was a giant metaphorical wall between them piled high with the dead bodies of his men and women.

He shook the thought off and ordered himself to be *professional*.

Adalyn gave him a warm smile that he would've believed if he'd been a stranger watching her. "Rick, this is Rae. She was on the van with us," she said as he sat on one of the thick wooden Adirondack-style chairs next to her. The chairs were in a circle around a huge stone-rimmed fire pit. Despite the icy Montana winter air, it was nice and toasty.

He nodded politely at the blonde who only gave him a tight smile.

Adalyn patted him gently on the knee, squeezed once, her eyes narrowing *ever so slightly*. "She and her husband are here for the same reasons we are," she said almost conspiratorially as she lowered her voice.

He blinked. *Uh, what?*

She continued. "It seems her husband cheated as well, but they're working through their issues and making a go of their marriage just like we are."

Cheated? He started to protest because he'd never cheated on anyone and never would, and if he had a woman like Adalyn, he'd— He stopped himself, however, because he certainly couldn't contradict her when she'd just added to their cover identity.

He gave a look he hoped appeared ashamed. "We've heard good things about this place and we're hoping to reconnect as I atone for my mistake," he said quietly, forcing himself not to grit his teeth.

Adalyn smiled sweetly at him and squeezed his knee again before turning back to the other woman, but he was pretty sure she was fighting a laugh. "So how long was your flight?" she asked the woman.

The banal question seemed to put Rae at ease and the two women fell into an easy conversation so he picked up her mostly half empty mug and murmured, "I'll get you a refresher." Then he looked at the other woman. "Did you want anything?"

"No, thank you," she murmured, not even sparing him a glance.

As he made his way to the outdoor bar, he saw Cash and Reese arriving, their arms wrapped around each other.

And he was pretty sure neither of them were exactly *acting*, at least not after the way he'd seen them run out of the wedding all over each other last weekend. As far as he knew, no one else knew or guessed that the two had hooked up, and he sure as hell wasn't going to tell anyone. He liked both of them and he hoped things worked out. For all their sakes. Because working with an ex was not fun, or at least he imagined it wouldn't be. And in their profession, they needed to be able to trust their partners... *Ah, hell.*

Of course Adalyn needed to know that he had her back. He had a whole lot of issues with her, but if the roles were reversed and she was stomping around like a giant dick, he'd be as pissed as she was. He needed to keep his shit together and get this job done right.

"It's Rick, right?" Cash, who was already waiting at the bar said as he approached to place his order. "Two hot cocoas. Fully loaded."

"We also have a fairly extensive bar if you would like anything else," the man behind the wood-hewn bar said.

"I'm good," Cash murmured.

"Same. And you're Cash, right?" Rowan asked, leaning into his role.

"Yep. These are some digs, right?" As always, Cash had an easy smile in place.

"I feel like the website undersold how impressive the cabins are," he said on a laugh.

Trailing off, Rowan turned as there was a soft rush of whispers then everyone quieted down. The owners, the Kingstons, were standing at the edge of the fire pit and smiling at everyone. He grabbed his and Adalyn's drinks and returned to the seating, Cash and Reese following.

Rowan noticed that Rae's husband hadn't arrived and frowned, looking around for the guy. She shouldn't be here alone.

Mila and Ben Kingston smiled at everyone, waiting for them to sit and settle before Mila spoke.

A tall, striking brunette in her forties, per her file, Mila wore dark jeans, worn-looking boots and what was likely a thick lamb's wool coat. Her husband was basically wearing the same thing, but he had on a Stetson. Her hair was pulled back in a tight braid.

"We're so glad to have a new group joining us this week," she said, beaming at them. "And I promise we'll keep things very short. We know y'all have had long flights and want to settle in and start relaxing. Breakfast is in the main cabin, but we also offer delivery to the cabins. There's no pressure for anyone to socialize. The only thing we ask is that if you decide to go on an unguided hike, you have to tell one of our employees and carry bear spray. We have patrols along our property but you're in the wilds of Montana. Bears and mountain lions are a very real thing. So be smart and be careful...and have fun!"

Her husband chimed in then, briefly going over some amenities before he said, "And that's it. Please enjoy getting to know your neighbors for the week or just sit back and relax. And always please let us or any one of our employees know if you need anything. We're a big family here."

Rowan watched as at least two employees rolled their eyes at Ben Kingston's declaration and bit back a smile. Usually in any corporate world, if someone described their coworkers as family, the place was toxic as hell. And yeah, he knew there was a lot of irony in him thinking that, considering he'd die for the people he worked with.

But his job wasn't a normal corporate nine-to-five.

By the time Ben Kingston finished talking, people were standing, some heading back to their cabins, including Cash and Reese. Though he got a text that said *Call when the two of you are alone* from Reese.

He texted back a thumbs-up then looked at Rae and Adalyn. "Unless you plan to hang out, we can walk you back to your cabin," he said to Rae, bothered that her husband just hadn't shown up.

"Ah..." She looked between the two of them. "It's not necessary, I promise. He probably just drank too much and fell asleep." There was a tired note in her voice that said it hadn't been the first time.

*Ahhh.* Well. "Humor us, then," he said, taking Adalyn's hand in his, not liking how well hers fit into his. "You heard what the owners said about bears."

The blonde shrugged and picked up her mug. "Thanks."

It didn't take long to walk her to her cabin, and only after they were alone and headed back to their own cabin, did he speak. "Cheating? Really?"

Adalyn's grin was pure Cheshire cat. "Figured we needed a good backstory and it makes me very sympathetic."

"I don't like it."

"Boo freaking hoo," she purred, still grinning.

And he had to look away from her because he liked that look on her way too much. He had to remind himself that he hated her, that because of her his people had gotten killed.

## Chapter 10

"If the wife knew about the affair, she could have gone after Aubry," Reese murmured as she stared at her laptop screen. They'd gotten back to the cabin not too long ago and had immediately done another dive into Mila and Ben Kingston. She and Gage had already done one over the previous week, creating files on everyone here, but nothing had stuck out in their phone records.

"The partners don't always know." Cash leaned back on the love seat, stretching his legs out in front of the crackling fireplace.

Reese tried not to pay attention to how long his legs were—how muscular she knew they were since she'd seen him without pants. Without *anything* on. "True enough." And she would know. "You ever get cheated on?" Okay...that was not the transition she'd been hoping for. *Smooth Reese, real smooth*, she chastised herself.

Cash blinked at her. "You're not going to ask if I'm a cheater?"

She snorted.

"What's that response?" He stretched his arms over the back of the couch as he got even more comfortable.

And she swore it was like he was stretching out for her benefit—showing off everything she so desperately wanted again. But wouldn't touch, because that way lay madness. "You're not a cheater," she finally said, then turned back to her screen as she continued to search for something useful they could use.

And if there was a money trail, she was going to follow it, because that never lied. People did stupid shit for cash every damn day. She and Gage hadn't found anything useful, but maybe they hadn't been looking in the right place. At least Elijah would be on this job. He'd been on vacation last week but he was back and she was looking forward to working with him, even if he'd be on the periphery.

Cash was silent for a long moment, the crackling of the fire and her fingertips on the keyboard the only sounds. Finally he spoke. "You're not wrong. I don't cheat. But yes, I've been cheated on."

"Your ex, the one from that gala?" Reese knew the woman's name was Isabella Vance—might have done a decent dive on the woman just out of uh, *curiosity*. Sure, yeah. She couldn't even lie to herself. Curiosity, jealousy, potato, potah-to. *Whatever*.

"I'm ninety-nine percent sure she did," he finally said on a sigh.

She glanced over and saw him watching her intently with those gorgeous green eyes she could drown in. "I'm sorry. I've been cheated on too. It sucks."

"Yeah...it does." He sat up in his seat, scrubbed his hands over his face, and she wondered if he held a torch for the woman.

Then she had to squash the green-eyed monster that wanted to come out and play. She wasn't a jealous person, never had been. And it wasn't like Cash was hers, but apparently he brought out something in her and she wasn't sure how she felt about it. Hell, how to deal with it. So she ignored it.

"So this is interesting," she murmured, her attention pulled back to her screen, but she paused when there was a soft knock at the back door.

Cash moved before she could even think about it, his large body all liquid grace, something that should be impossible for someone so big. "Probably Joelle," he said, his legs eating up the distance to the back door in seconds.

Reese closed her laptop on instinct and slid it under a throw pillow—not that anyone here could likely get into her laptop anyway. Not with the security she had, but old habits and all that.

Joelle stepped in with a bundle of towels and what was surely champagne in one of those chilled holders. "Hi," she whispered, even though it was just the two of them here.

Cash immediately took the stuff from her and shut the door behind her.

The back of the cabin was basically all windows, even the doors being glass, but there were automatic blinds and they'd closed themselves in for privacy.

"There's some more stuff I need to tell you guys," Joelle said, moving into the living room, standing near the fireplace. "I just... I feel weird I guess." She tucked a strand of her blonde hair behind her ear, then tugged off her thick-looking purple gloves.

"Why don't you sit?" Cash motioned to the nearby cushioned chair. "The windows are all closed and no one can see. And we already swept this place for bugs."

Joelle looked startled by that, but then seemed to gather herself and sat.

"Anything you say is between us. We're here to help, that's it. We want to find your friend."

Joelle nodded, biting her bottom lip. "I know, and I'm so grateful. I guess this whole situation just feels weird. I've never dealt with this before and the sheriff's department just blew me off. I'm... I just want to find my friend."

"Of course you do," Reese murmured, keeping her voice low, soft as she tried to coax the woman into opening up. "Earlier you said that Aubry was seeing Mr. Kingston?"

The young woman nodded, looking miserable. "Yeah. I mean, I'm pretty sure it was him. I saw the way he looked at her and..." She shoved out a sigh. "I've heard rumors that he's hooked up with other employees. Like before I got here, not anyone else I know."

"Do you have any names?" Reese asked, even though she'd just gotten a hit on some interesting information, including the names of former employees—and two who looked similar to Aubry Boyle.

"Ah, no, but I can find out."

Cash shook his head before Reese could say anything. "No, don't worry about that. We'll figure out what's important and what's not."

"Okay well, I wanted to let you know that Mrs. Kingston leaves every Wednesday morning. Supposedly it's for some standing doctor's appointment but...maybe it's important? She's gone for a few hours and comes back right around lunchtime like clockwork. And I know I said it before, but their offices are off-limits, which makes sense. But Mr. Kingston is really, really weird about anyone being in there. One of our ranch hands dropped something off once and rumor is, Mr. Kingston lost his shit. Almost fired the guy just for going in there. Accused him of breaking in, but apparently Mrs. Kingston had left it unlocked. The whole thing was so overblown, but everyone stays away from their office now. It could be nothing, but it's just weird."

*Weird, indeed.* "Did Aubry ever talk about a special place she met up with her boyfriend or anything?"

Joelle shook her head, her blonde ponytail swishing slightly. "No, not really. I mean, sometimes she would go hiking alone in the spring and brush off attempts when I asked to join, but always in a nice way. She would talk about how she wanted time with her thoughts." The woman shrugged.

"Has anyone been in her cabin since she went missing?"

"Ah, to clean, sure, but no one is in there, if that's what you mean?"

"Can you get us a key?" Reese asked, even though they could easily break in. It would still be faster with a key.

"Sure, but I don't think you'll find anything."

"We probably won't, but we like to cover all our bases," Cash added smoothly, throwing in that charming smile Reese wasn't sure she'd ever get used to.

And Joelle definitely wasn't unaffected, if her slight blush was any indication. "Okay, I'll get it for you. Tonight?"

"No, just sometime tomorrow. Do you happen to know which trails Aubry liked to hike?"

"Yeah."

"Can you get a list of all of them?" he asked.

"Of course."

"If you're comfortable, just text them to us," Reese added.

"I will. I'm... so shaken up with her missing. Because I know she didn't go home." Her jaw tightened. "And if Mr. Kingston had anything to do with her disappearance, he deserves to go to jail."

Reese nodded. "We're going to do everything we can to find your friend." Unfortunately, Reese was fairly certain it was too late for the woman. But she deserved justice if that was the case, and her family deserved to bury their daughter.

Once Joelle was gone, Cash put the champagne in the refrigerator as Reese pulled her laptop back out. "I found something interesting—names of former employees over the last five years who fall into the same age range as Aubry Boyle, and they're all similar in looks. Petite brunettes with big, innocent smiles. They all ended their employment just shy of a year and..." Feeling proud of herself, she turned her laptop around, let him look at the multiple screens. "Two of them got what I would describe as a payoff, given the huge chunk, and this third one is getting monthly payments from an anonymous account. We didn't see this during our first run of information because they're not current employees.

"Four grand a month," Cash said thoughtfully. "And no payoff for this one, just the monthly payments."

"Almost fifty grand a year for the last two years and counting. She's going to come out ahead of the others eventually if the payments keep up. And," Reese turned her laptop back to herself and leaned back on the couch, "she's only two hours away."

"You think we should talk to her?"

"I want to see what we can find here, but yeah. The others are too far away, and if they were paid off, they likely signed NDAs. Eventually I'd like to reach out to them, but Mia Williams is close. We can drive there and be back easily."

"How are we going to do that?"

"Elijah is getting us a truck and is going to have someone stash it where we can use it."

Cash blinked in surprise. "Seriously?"

"Yep. Someone will tuck it away on the edge of this property, near the highway. We'll have to hike to use it, but you've seen the satellite images. There are a lot of trails here." Which made searching for someone damn near impossible. And hiding a body way too easy.

"Who owns the bank account?" Cash asked, switching subjects as he sat next to her—far too close for comfort.

This close, she could smell his sandalwood and sage cologne and she wanted to bury her face in his neck. Or...other places. *Gah!* She had to get her mind far, far away from there. It was just so hard when he was right up against her and she remembered exactly how he'd felt sliding inside her, stretching her.

The man was big everywhere and she most definitely wanted a repeat. Because pretending that they'd never seen each other naked, that she'd never seen, heard and felt him climax—and vice versa—was becoming harder and harder.

"Ah...I'm not sure yet," she said, remembering he'd asked her a question that did not involve taking off their clothes. "But I'll find out who. I always do."

"I believe you," he murmured, his heated gaze falling to her mouth before he abruptly stood. "If you don't need my help, I'm going to grab a quick shower."

"I'm good. I just want to look into a few things but I'll be up soon." Where they would apparently be sharing a bed. Right? Unless he was going to sleep on the couch or floor or something.

Which, no, that was ridiculous. Especially since they were undercover. They had to be in their roles at all times.

*\*\*\**

Cash stepped into the living room, found Reese with her laptop in front of her, and her head firmly on the cushion behind her.

Moving quietly, he slid her laptop to the table, then scooped her up in his arms.

Her eyes flew open and she blinked as he headed for the stairs. "What..." Blearily, she glanced around.

"You're not sleeping on the couch."

"I wasn't sleeping," she murmured, leaning her head on his shoulder.

He snorted softly. "Okay. Well you're not napping on the couch."

"I was working...with my eyes closed. I'm good at it. Don't be jealous of my talent." Her words were thick with sleep, but he could hear the amusement in her voice.

"I'll try to contain my jealousy." He kept his voice low as he eased her into bed. Forget about sleep clothes or...maybe she slept naked? She had, the night they'd spent together, but he wasn't certain that was the norm for her. Though a man could hope.

"I found some interesting stuff on the employees who left," she continued, her eyes still shut as she curled up on the pillow.

"You want to change?" he asked.

"No. Because I'm not sleeping. Just closing my eyes."

"I'm going to close my eyes with you, then," he murmured, sliding into bed behind her. And because he wanted to hold her, he moved in behind her and wrapped his arm around her.

"What are you doing?"

"I'm cold. You can keep me warm."

She snorted in a very Reese-like manner and patted his arm as she pulled him tighter. "Fine. But just for tonight." Her words trailed off as she fell into slumber.

He shut his own eyes, wondering...how the hell he was going to work with this woman who drove him absolutely mad.

She was just pretending like the other night hadn't happened, as if she hadn't blown up his entire world. Because the sex had been off the charts, but it was more than that. He flat-out liked Reese Sinclair to the point of distraction.

He'd never wanted someone the way he wanted her—obsessed about her, if he was being brutally honest with himself. Women had been throwing themselves at him for as long as he could remember. Back when he'd had nothing, then after he'd started making money, he'd been like a magnet.

And he'd fallen for the wrong woman, someone who hadn't been real at all. He certainly hadn't been looking for a relationship when he'd met Reese, but that was what he wanted now.

He just had to figure out how to convince her that he was more than just a good time in bed. Though...he wanted a hell of a lot more time in bed as well. Or on the floor, against a wall, in the shower. He wasn't picky.

As long as they were both naked.

## Chapter 11

Reese opened her eyes into a rock-hard wall of warmth...Cash's chest. Ooooh yeah, he'd carried her to bed last night. Or more likely this morning. She had no idea what time she'd dozed off before he'd hauled her upstairs.

In his big-ass arms. Jesus, the man was strong. And oh, he smelled so good. She leaned forward, pressed her nose to his very bare chest and subtly inhaled. Yep, sandalwood and sage.

"Are you smelling me?" Cash's deep, sleep-laden voice rumbled around them.

Uh oh, *busted*. "You smell good." Why deny it?

"I taste even better."

She blinked as a wave of heat unfurled inside her. He really, really did. And that night they'd had together had been so good. Okay, great, incredible, *incendiary* and a bunch of other adjectives that barely scraped the surface of how he'd made her feel. "That's...beside the point."

Another rumble came from him and she realized he was laughing. "I don't think it is."

She pulled back slightly, though she immediately missed his warmth, and met his very intense gaze. "We've got work to do," she whispered, her eyes falling to his mouth. And just like that, memories of the way she'd sat on his face and he'd made her come with that wicked mouth and tongue bombarded her.

"Breakfast doesn't start for another hour."

Oh, so they were up pretty early. Still... "Well I need to shower." Because she'd slept in her clothes. But she couldn't seem to pull away.

Until he removed the thick comforter that had somehow gotten tangled between their lower bodies and she felt his erection. Oh god, he was just as thick and hard as she remembered.

Seeing that he was so turned on was a slap of reality, jerking her entirely from sleep. She eased back. "I'm going to grab a quick shower. I think...we should just..." Clearing her throat, she slid from the bed and mumbled nonsensical words.

But she didn't miss him call out "coward" as she shut the bathroom door behind her.

Was she a coward? Yep. The sand was warm where she'd buried her head. Just the way she liked it. She'd been burned before by men she barely cared for. Not the way she did Cash. The men she'd been with before had all been more or less "projects," which was embarrassing to admit. She hadn't actually thought of them that way at the time, but after therapy and self-reflection...she'd certainly had a type before.

Now, her only type was the unattainable Cash Pierce. A man who would eventually see right through her and break her heart.

So she was simply playing it safe, doing the only sane thing—keeping things professional between them.

Strictly. Professional.

*So stop imagining his gorgeous dick. Ugh.*

She stepped into the freezing shower and bit back a yelp because it was just the wake-up she needed. The reminder that she didn't need to do something stupid and blow up her life. But one taste of him hadn't been enough.

"Well it better be," she muttered to herself as the water slowly heated up. "No more fun for you," she continued, looking down the length of her body and realized that yep, she was talking to her vagina.

Which was about as weird as she was going to get for the day.

\*\*\*

"You look gorgeous. I like the snow bunny look," Cash said as Reese stepped into the living room.

Where he was already waiting—looking gorgeous himself. He had on dark jeans, hiking boots and a thick coat that was probably sheepskin or something. It looked like one of those bomber jackets that ranchers on TV wore and... She realized she was staring. "Ah, thanks, you look very nice too." In contrast to him, she was wearing a thick, puffy purple jacket, a sparkly toque a few shades lighter to keep her ears warm, tight black pants lined with fleece, and flashy hiking boots—with pops of purple—that were part of her cover. Her real hiking boots at home were well worn and comfortable, but as the "fiancée" of a wealthy man, she wanted to look like the kind of woman who took winter vacations with her man in Aspen, Telluride and Verbier if they were in Switzerland.

"Nice?" He lifted a dark eyebrow.

"I'm not inflating your ego—and just forget I said the word inflate!" she snapped when his mouth kicked up in an obnoxious grin. God, he really was gorgeous, especially when he smiled. So...all the time, basically.

"I was simply going to say I made you coffee the way you like it," he murmured. "And you can feel free to inflate any part of—"

"Cash!" She stomped over to the island in the kitchen, which was connected to the living room since this part of the cabin was all open concept. She lifted her to-go mug and inhaled. "They had the creamer I like?"

"I ordered it while you were in the shower. Someone else brought it, not Joelle."

"Oh. Well thank you. That's very sweet."

"That's what you get with Cash Pierce. A sweet, giving boyfriend."

She nearly choked on her coffee, but managed to cover it up. Sort of. She refused to let him get under her skin.

"Oh, I also grabbed this." He took her left hand and slid her faux engagement ring on her left-hand ring finger.

A shiver rolled through her at the contact, especially when he held her hand for a bit too long, rubbing his thumb over her palm before he dropped her hand. And damn, did she like the way the ring looked on her finger waaaaay too much. Her gaze flicked to his own hand, and to her surprise, he had on a ring. "You're wearing a ring?"

He lifted a broad shoulder. "I figure it makes a statement that I'm off the market." And god, with that grin of his, she felt her knees getting ridiculously weak again.

She cleared her throat, wanting to stay on task even though she loved the idea of him being off the market, only hers. *Get it together, Sinclair!* she silently ordered herself. "Okay so last night I found all the social media accounts of the women we think might have been paid off. I'm using one of our burner/cover accounts and have already reached out to two of them. I also reached out to Mia Williams so hopefully we'll hear back from her."

Cash blinked in surprise. "When did you do that?"

"Before I passed out on the couch." Before he'd carried her upstairs and she'd spent the night cuddling with him like a total masochist. "Oh and Elijah also told me that he's got someone dropping off a vehicle soon. He'll drop us a pin to the location once it's done."

"Yeah, I know, already talked to him this morning."

*Oh, right.* "Good. So...are you ready?"

"Ready to be your loving, affectionate fiancé while we sneak around this place? Definitely."

She bit back a grin because she wasn't going to encourage him. Even if the man was adorable. "Glad you're so excited. During breakfast I'm going to see if I can hack into and clone either or both of the owners' phones. If I can isolate them, that is." She needed to be close enough to them. They also planned to feel out some of the employees about the missing woman, break into the owners' office, and plant cameras and listening devices in areas they might overhear anything useful. Having eyes and ears on the ground was often the best thing they could do in an investigation because people talked when they assumed they were alone.

But planting cameras without being seen was the tricky part. She'd done it on previous jobs, though usually one of the guys handled that. And this would be Cash's first op. Though she had no doubt he'd be able to handle himself. The man seemed to excel at everything he did. It was just a matter of the two of them working together and finding a rhythm. Not to mention they had Rowan and Adalyn with them. At least Rowan was a known quantity, even if he'd been off-kilter the last week.

"You got everything in your pack?" he asked, glancing at her little backpack that looked more fashionable than useful. The backpack was puffy like her jacket, but bright white with a unicorn skiing on the main pocket. It was kind of ridiculous, but Reese was going to keep it after this job because it was adorable, and she liked ridiculous most of the time. Inside was where the good stuff was—all the tools they needed for today.

"Yep. I'm ready to go if you are."

He nodded and as they stepped onto the back porch, he took her gloved hand in his. Even without skin-to-skin contact, she felt his touch to her core, knew how easy she could fall into something with him. But she also knew that they were too different—and they now worked together. Getting tangled up with him was just monumentally stupid.

As they headed down the path between the huge cabins, she saw that most of the blinds were still closed over windows. A lot of people would be sleeping in or ordering breakfast in, she guessed. Which made sense, if the point was to reconnect with your partner. There were only a couple classes early this morning: a yoga one and a meditation one. Neither of which they were attending.

She hoped the breakfast was sparsely attended and that the owners showed up...

"Hey," she murmured as she spotted none other than Ben Kingston turn onto their path in front of them.

He was walking at a brisk pace, no Stetson on this morning, revealing a thick head of blond hair. In the same coat as the night before and a pair of jeans and boots, it was definitely him. And he seemed to be on a mission, given his steady pace.

"Want to head in his direction?" Cash murmured even though he was about forty yards ahead of them and wouldn't be able to hear them.

"Yeah. We can just pretend we got lost if anyone wonders what we're doing." She kept her voice just as low.

Glancing around, she looked at the cabins as they passed, saw most had lights on even if the blinds were closed. The roads between the cabins were paved, but not wide enough for cars or trucks. Four-wheelers or ATVs could easily move through here and she was certain that was what the employees used when getting around. As they passed the path they were supposed to turn off toward the dining hall, both she and Cash glanced in that direction, saw two couples walking toward where they'd been instructed.

Kingston continued down the path, then veered off onto a gravel path with a sign that said *Sunshine Trail, 3.4 miles*. Underneath it was an image of the actual shape of the trail.

"Want to follow?" Cash murmured. "I've got bear spray on me."

She nodded. "Yeah. Maybe he's going for a walk, or maybe he's meeting someone. Either way, if we can get close enough, I can try to clone his phone." Just depended on the man's encryption. She pulled out her cell phone and opened up the program she needed to run, then texted Elijah and Gage, told them what she was doing.

"Is it crazy to attempt to plant cameras out here?" Cash asked quietly as he scanned either side of the trail, which was just thick trees.

According to the image, there was supposed to be a lake or creek nearby.

"Not crazy, no, but...maybe not useful." Today they were going to plant cameras in the dining area, all the outdoor bars, the spa and maybe one of the barns if possible. "This trail is almost four miles, but if you want to..." She trailed off as they rounded the bend in the path and saw Mr. Kingston ducking off the main path into a thick cluster of woods.

Cash moved in front of her, automatically she guessed, and gently pushed her behind him. Which was...ugh, wonderful. She loved how protective he was, even if she didn't need it.

At the sound of an engine flaring to life, they took a few steps toward the noise, but then it immediately faded in the distance.

Without a word, the two of them took off down the trail, only stopping where Kingston had ducked into the woods...and saw another little trail only big enough for a four-wheeler.

They looked at the tire tracks in the snow and Reese bit back a curse. "I don't think he saw us."

"No, he didn't," Cash murmured in agreement. "This was preplanned... Want to follow?"

"He's on a four-wheeler, we're on foot with no visual or idea where he's gone... No. Let's just stick to the plan and plant the cameras this morning. If anything, this is good because he's not in his office now."

Cash's eyes lit up at that. "You want to skip breakfast and break in?"

"I don't think it would hurt to try," she said, already pulling up her phone to text Rowan and Adalyn. "I can bring the security cameras down for at least ten minutes and give me enough time to break in, but we'll need to make sure the wife is busy."

"I'm great at distractions." Cash grinned, making him look young and adorable, but the glint in his green eyes gave away his age, the things he'd seen. This was a man who'd been to war, a man who'd definitely killed.

She hadn't seen his résumé, hadn't wanted to snoop even though she totally could have. But despite his sweetness, there was a lot more to Cash Pierce.

And she hated that she wanted to peel back all his layers, wanted to know all of him. Because she wasn't supposed to care so much, wasn't supposed to care at all. And now she'd dug herself a hole because every second of every day, her curiosity for this man grew.

Screw curiosity, she wanted him with every fiber of her being and it was worse because she knew exactly how amazing they were together. But physical hunger eventually waned, she reminded herself. And that was even if he didn't ditch her before then.

## CHAPTER 12

Reese drilled a tiny hole into one of the frames on the wall before sliding the mini camera inside. Once it was secure, she moved to the next spot, an 8x10 frame on one of the bookshelves. Hiding the cameras was easy enough, especially since her drill was quiet and the owners' office was on the outskirts of everything.

The only bad thing was she'd had to trek through the woods to sneak in from one of the windows—after temporarily taking down their security cameras. She could have knocked it out for good, but they wanted to make it look like a glitch relating to weather.

"You've got about five minutes," Rowan said into her earpiece. "Cash and the wife are headed your way."

"Packing up now," she murmured, tucking the drill into her kit. She'd placed three cameras total, which was enough for a space this small, but she'd have liked to have dug around in the office more thoroughly.

It seemed these people weren't huge on using their computer, from what she'd found—the password had been written on a Post-it and tossed into one of the top drawers of the desk. She'd downloaded everything and now had a back door into the computer, but at first glance there wasn't anything but business stuff on it.

And most of their résumés were in actual paper format in their filing cabinet. Which was wild to her. But she'd managed to scan a few images to go over later.

As she slid her backpack on, saw she had two minutes to spare, the door handle jingled.

*What. The. Hell.*

"Someone's here," she said so quietly she wasn't sure Rowan would overhear her, but panic punched through her even as she forced herself to remain calm.

"What? Oh shit. I'm on the way."

Reese didn't respond because she couldn't. She'd been in tough spots before. Opening the window would make too much noise and there wasn't enough cover for her to run—and with all the purple she was wearing, anyone would be able to point her out of a crowd easily.

"Come on," someone grumbled at the sound of keys rustling.

Moving quickly, her heart pounding, she pulled out what looked like a deflated blow-up Christmas decoration from the side of one of the metal filing cabinets. Then she squeezed in between the cabinet and the wall and pulled the brown material in front of her, using it as a cover. What was this thing anyway? A moose or maybe a reindeer? One of the eyes was looking at her as she remained very, very still.

The door swung open with a bang, hitting the nearby filing cabinet and rattling the entire thing.

She would have jumped, but couldn't move, was barely fitting into the space as it was.

"Where is it?" a male voice murmured and it took her a moment to realize he was talking to himself when no one answered. Thankfully he was alone.

There was some rustling of papers, then silence and she thought for sure she'd been busted. Had she left something behind? Her drill? Her toque, oh god... No, that was on her head. And her mini backpack was squeezed into this spot with her.

"Oh, honey, what are you doing here?" A female voice now, definitely Mila Kingston. "I thought you were meeting with one of the contractors."

"Ah, we moved it to later today," Ben Kingston said.

"Oh, okay, well this is Mr. Pierce. We started talking at breakfast and he's interested in donating to the wildlife sanctuary we're building. I wanted to bring him here for some privacy but I didn't realize how messy everything was," she said with what sounded like a self-deprecating laugh.

"It's fine. You should see my office at home." Cash's deep voice soothed her, grounded her, even though she could be caught at any moment.

There was a short bit of laughter from the couple, then Ben Kingston cleared his throat. "I'll leave you guys to it. I got a text from Henry anyway. Some issue with some of the security cameras. I'm going to go check it out."

The door shut, then Mila Kingston spoke again. "Why don't you take a seat?"

"Ah, thanks, but I won't take up much of your time. I'm supposed to meet up with my fiancée for a couples massage soon."

"Well you're both in for a treat," she murmured to the sound of a drawer being opened. "Lauren and Evan are great."

"A friend of mine recommended we hit up some of the trails as well. Said a woman named Aubry was a great guide." Cash's tone was light, easy.

"Aubry left us not too long ago." Mila Kingston's voice was just as easy. "I was really sad to see her go, but she wanted to move back home to be closer to family. Now here's a brief outline of what we've started and what we're hoping to do. It's important to me—ah, to both of us, to preserve the land around us. I'm actually from here and I want to do everything possible to maintain the integrity of what we're doing here."

"I love that you're doing that." Cash's voice was easy, relaxed.

Reese was as still as a statue as they continued talking, until finally Cash said, "I need to meet up with my fiancée but I'll definitely reach out about this. Would you mind walking out with me and pointing me in the right direction? This place is pretty big."

"Of course," Mila said on a laugh.

After the sound of chairs scraping on wood, then the door opening and closing, Reese moved fast, wincing as she wiggled her way out of the tight space. With trembling fingers, she shoved the blow-up thing back in the space then opened the nearest window. It creaked loudly as she slid it up and she winced again, hoping they were too far away to hear it.

"I'm heading out the window," she whispered to Rowan.

"Cash is out front with the wife. You're good."

Relief punched through her as she crawled out the window and landed in a snow-covered bush. But she managed to get the window shut—the lock would just have to stay unlocked. "I'm fully out."

"Head to the east side of the office and use the line of ATVs as cover. Her back is to you anyway. And Cash is still talking to her. You're good."

She peered around the side of the exterior wall, saw that Cash had his hands shoved into his jacket pockets as he nodded at something the tall brunette said.

Trusting her team, Reese sprinted to the nearest ATV and used each one as cover until she could dart into the woods.

"Cameras are up and look good." Adalyn spoke for the first time through the feed. "I've got clear visuals in the office."

"Good. I've got to meet Cash for the massage but then we'll rendezvous in the meeting spot. I'll tag you if we're able to install cameras in the spa."

"Sounds good. See you then," Rowan said.

Reese slid her earpiece out as she hurried through the woods, her heart rate not quite back to normal until she made it back to the trail she'd used to get to the office. As she backtracked, she pulled her hood over her head as a gust of icy wind rolled over her. Yeah, she wasn't cut out for this kind of weather. But at least her winter gear was heavily insulated.

At the end of the trail, she checked her cell phone, saw a message from Cash telling her that he was waiting for her at the spa center.

*Two minutes away*, she texted back, picking up her pace. There was no one on the trail now probably because it was overcast and people were getting all oiled up and massaged—or whatever else.

As she made it to one of the main pathways, a man in an ATV pulled up and tugged his face covering down. "Were you out hiking?" he asked even as he motioned for her to get in.

"Oh, no, I just wanted to grab a picture of the beginning of the trail for my sister," Reese lied as she slid into the front seat. She was surprised to find the seat was heated. "I'm meeting up with my fiancé to get a massage. This cold is way too much for me," she continued, hoping he'd ignore her if she chattered on.

"Okay, well good." The guy pulled his face covering back in place. "You've always got to take a partner and let someone know if you go out on any of the trails. And it's supposed to snow soon so I don't recommend it anyway."

"No arguments from me," she said on a laugh. "Would you mind dropping me off at Cabin F?"

"No problem. How are you liking your stay so far?" he asked as he steered down another road, this one lined with the spa cabins, A through H.

"The amenities are great," she said, her eyes widening as she spotted Mr. Kingston and a bundled-up brunette standing in between cabins E and F having what looked like a heated conversation. Not wanting to get caught staring she glanced ahead as her driver pulled in front of cabin F. "How long have you worked here?"

"Not long, just about eight months. Remember, if you need a ride anywhere, they should have given you a number to text when you arrived. Someone will pick you up and drop you off anywhere you want to go."

It was probably in the welcome kit, but she nodded like she remembered. "Will do, thanks." She smiled to see Cash already waiting for her at the top of the stairs.

Then she cursed herself for her reaction, for the little flutters inside her at the mere sight of him. *Ugh.* She was so screwed.

***

"You're sure you're good?" Cash whispered after they were alone in the massage room.

Someone had given them water, asked if they wanted more refreshments, then shown them to the private room where their masseurs would be joining them soon.

The scents of lavender, tea tree and something else she couldn't pinpoint filled the air. Soft instrumental music played from discreet speakers and there were two sheet-covered tables with donut-hole-style pillows for them to put their faces in. "Yeah," she said, moving quickly with her pack.

They would have about five minutes before the massage team returned and they would be expected to be stripped and on the table facedown under the sheet.

"I don't like placing these in such a public area," Cash murmured as she handed him two tiny cameras—no drilling for these.

"I don't either," she admitted. "But we'll fully erase everything after the job. And we're only listening to the employees talking, not recording anyone stripping or anything," she continued as she secured one of the cameras near the top of one of the heavy armoire-type cabinets that held towels.

If someone was looking right at it, they might see it, but they blended well with the dark wood. She really did hate this part of her job because it felt like a violation of privacy, but employees talked freely with each other and it could give them information they might not otherwise have.

As soon as she'd placed another camera, this one on a lower cabinet filled with towels and oils, she shelved her self-consciousness and started stripping.

Cash looked startled, but then he tugged his sweater, then T-shirt off. "Is this your first massage?" he asked as they both stripped down to their underwear.

She laughed lightly. "No, how about you?"

"Nah. A guy I worked with told me about hot stone massages and I thought he was messing with me. But turned out, he wasn't and I love them. I have back issues and they really help. Not that I broadcast the fact that I get them with an embarrassing regularity."

She snickered slightly even as she took her bra off. "Is your image too manly for massages?"

He avoided looking at her breasts as he slid onto the table facedown—he kept his underwear on too, she noticed. "I don't know, it feels kind of obnoxious to get them so often."

"Maybe, maybe not." She got on the table, shivered even with the warmth of the room. "It sounds like they help you physically and it's good to take care of yourself, physically, mentally, all of the above. I know people can be judgmental assholes—and I'm including myself in that because I know I can be judgy sometimes and I'm working on it—but there's nothing wrong with taking care of yourself."

Cash had started to say something when there was a knock on the door, then a female voice said, "Are you ready for us?"

"We're ready," she murmured then looked up as two people walked in. The college-age brunette she'd seen outside talking to Ben Kingston and a man who looked the same age.

"Hi, I'm Lauren and this is Evan. We've looked over your questionnaire and we'll be using the essential oils you've chosen. Reese, I'll be massaging you with a standard Swedish massage, and it looks like Evan will be doing a stone massage for you...Cash." She stumbled on his name, which made Reese smother a grin. "If there are any particular problem areas, please let us know, or if you want to stop at any moment for any reason, also let us know.

"All that sounds good," Reese said, answering, when Cash simply stuck his head in the face cushion.

She'd hoped to question the woman some but it was clear this wasn't the right place for that. Sometimes when she got massages, the masseurs liked to talk, but it was obvious that these two were pros as Evan quietly murmured to Cash asking about the temperature of the stones, and Lauren simply started working on her upper back with practiced efficiency.

Reese forced herself to relax, even if it felt weird to be enjoying a massage in the middle of the job. And at that thought, she wondered what it would be like to have Cash's very capable hands massaging her in a very different place.

*Nope. No time for that.* Not now, not ever, she reminded herself.

# Chapter 13

"Just take your time getting dressed," Lauren said to both Cash and Reese as the two massage therapists stepped outside. "We'll have cucumber water waiting for you when you're done."

Keeping the sheet over her chest, Reese rolled over to find Cash already sitting up, his sheet loosely in place. "I feel like I'm high," she whispered.

He grinned. "Same. And I feel guilty doing this in the middle of..." He cleared his throat, that smile dimming a bit.

"Same. And don't." She glanced toward the door, then hurried to her backpack. Working quickly, she used one of her special programs to "cast" for other devices and... "Bingo."

"I know that look well enough," Cash murmured as he tugged his pants on.

And she had to make herself not watch as he got dressed, because she was a professional. *Not* a pervert.

"You can look all you want," he said as if he'd read her mind.

Her gaze snapped to his. "Well you can't."

"Too late. Not that it matters," he whispered, stalking toward her—shirtless. "Because the image of you naked, underneath me, calling out my name as you climax, is forever seared into my brain."

Heat punched through her, but just as quickly... "Rowan and Adalyn have eyes and ears on this room."

He blinked, winced, then, "Shit."

"Yeah that about sums it up." So she was going to pretend that no one was listening, and who knew, maybe they weren't? They were only supposed to watch the feeds when it was the employees in here talking. *Ugh.*

"I'll stand in front of you while you dress," he finally said, turning around.

She doubted the other two were watching them change, like perverts, but she was still moved by the gesture. On instinct, she reached out to touch Cash's back, but drew her hand away before quickly dressing. As she pulled her sweater over her head, she whispered, "I cloned Lauren's phone. I saw her having a very heated conversation with Ben Kingston. We might be able to scrape something from it." That was the hope anyway.

Anything that could point them in the right direction to tell them what had happened to Aubry Boyle. Where she was, if...she was still alive.

"I'm ready."

Cash nodded and finished getting dressed, but was quiet until they'd fully left the cabin.

As soon as they were outside, back in the freezing cold, he took her hand in his, maybe as part of his cover. "I'm really sorry about back there. I...I need to get used to being monitored. I know it's part of the job sometimes. I wasn't thinking. It was completely unprofessional—"

She tugged him to a stop, and when he turned toward her, she took his face in her hands. Before she'd even moved up on tiptoe, he'd crushed his mouth to hers in a searing kiss she felt all the way to her toes and then some.

It felt like he was claiming her. And oh sweet flying pandas, heat curled inside her, warming her from the inside out as he teased his tongue against hers, reminding her of exactly how he'd teased between her legs with such thoroughness that she'd come on his face more than once.

Slowly, he lifted his head from her and she had to order herself to move. To not just stand there like a statue. "I just..." She couldn't even remember why she'd started the kiss. Oh right, because she'd wanted to. No...he'd been beating himself up and she simply couldn't stand that. He hadn't done anything wrong. She cleared her throat. "Well then."

Cash looked as if he was going to say something, but her phone buzzed in her pocket. And when she saw the message, hope jumped inside her.

"We might have a lead," she murmured, holding out her phone so he could read the email. It was from Mia Williams.

The response was short and to the point. *I can meet up at Starlight Café but my window is small. I'll be there at 3 today and can talk for fifteen minutes. If you can meet me, fine. If not, this is the only time that works for my schedule.* —M

Cash lifted an eyebrow. "That's very abrupt."

"Yeah." Reese fell in step with them as they headed back to their cabin. She'd return the message as soon as they had privacy. "But she responded, which means she's curious enough to meet. That alone is interesting."

There were more people out and about now, using the services, but this wasn't a packed retreat, which was part of the appeal of the place. There were only twenty couples here at a given time, according to the website and what the owners had spouted at the meet and greet last night.

"What did you say to her anyway?"

"I was pretty blunt, figuring it would be better. I said I'd had a relationship with the same person she had," she murmured even though no one was close enough to overhear them. "And that same person offered me a payoff and I was curious if she'd talk to me about it."

"Damn, that is blunt."

"Given her response, I think it ended up being the right move."

Instead of heading to their cabin, they went straight to Rowan and Adalyn's. Reese really, really hoped the other two hadn't heard their little conversation or at least pretended like they hadn't.

Adalyn opened the back door for them and motioned for them to step inside. Most of their blinds were down, but there was enough natural light from some of the higher windows that the place didn't feel stifled. The ceilings were too high for that anyway. She saw that the interior was simple, with comfortable but high-end couches, a huge fireplace, what looked like local art on all the walls and a state-of-the-art kitchen.

"Mia Williams responded and is willing to meet," Reese said by way of greeting because they had very limited time to make this work. "Which means I need to get off this property—"

"We," Cash said, collapsing on one of the couches in the living room.

"We?"

"Yeah, we. You're not going alone."

"It'll be easier for one person to sneak out—"

"Nope, no sneaking." Cash shook his head. "Or not too much. We're going to report in that we're going on a hike and we'll hoof it to the truck Elijah planted for us. Then a couple hours later we'll report in that we're done with our hike and will be staying in our room for a while. No one will need to actually see us return. We can even bring Joelle in to help us. Not that I think anyone is going to question us given how relaxed this place is, but she can drop off more champagne or something and sell our story if needed that we're taking alone time."

"Worst case scenario, if someone realizes you're not in your cabin, we'll just say you came to our place for an orgy," Rowan said. "Or a couple swap. Whatever. We'll sell it."

Reese blinked. "You pulled that out of your back pocket pretty quick."

"You should always have back up orgy plans ready to go," Cash said.

She looked up at him in horror. "I don't even know how to respond to that."

"Don't respond. He's a moron." Adalyn's tone was dry.

"I won't argue with you there," Reese murmured in agreement, even as she bit back a laugh.

## Chapter 14

"I can't believe you're okay with me driving," Cash said as they cruised down the two-lane highway. It hadn't taken long to get to the well-hidden truck and be on their way.

"I hate driving in snowy or icy conditions." Reese didn't look up from her laptop as she answered.

She seemed totally immune to the kiss they'd shared earlier, and it was all he could think about. Well, that and getting her naked again. "Find anything interesting?"

"Maybe... Mia Williams's social media is different than the other women I contacted. She's got one for work, but nothing personal. Like...not even a hint of personal, which is maybe not odd, but not quite the norm."

"You and I don't have social media accounts. Not real ones anyway."

"Yeah, well, unless she's secretly Batman or whatever, then her not having any personal social media is interesting."

"What does her work stuff look like?"

"It's basically a portfolio of her art. She's good too. I might buy one of her pieces." There was a note of awe in Reese's voice.

"Send me a link, I want to check out her stuff if she's that good."

"I will...huh."

That *huh* sounded very interesting, but Cash remained quiet as Reese continued working, muttering to herself.

"Okay, so this is interesting. Her taxes list a dependent."

"She has a kid?"

"She didn't a couple years ago, but...hold on."

That "hold on" turned into half an hour so Cash turned the radio on low as he drove through another quiet, rural town. There was so much damn land and open space here, and while he had a small ranch in Virginia, the ranches here were a lot more isolated. Everything here felt like they were on a different planet almost.

But as the speed limit slowed to forty-five miles per hour, and a sign displayed their upcoming destination as only three miles away, more signs of life popped into view. Gas stations, a coffee shop, a nursery.

Then the shops got a lot closer together and a quaint mountain town bustling with a lot more life than the last town they'd driven through spread out around them. Brick buildings no more than three stories lined the main strip, with vehicles parked in front of every shop. There were people walking, all bundled up in winter gear, some with dogs or kids, or couples holding hands. And the backdrop to it was a cluster of snow-topped mountains he was certain had ended up on thousands of postcards. It was like driving onto a Hallmark set.

"According to the GPS, we're about a third of a mile from the café so I'm going to park here," he said as he steered into one of the last spots in front of a breakfast diner.

Reese closed her laptop, her eyes slightly wide as he put the vehicle in park. "Mia Williams had a kid about six months after she left her employment with the Kingstons, and I'm pretty sure that Ben Kingston is the father."

# Chapter 15

Reese spotted Mia before she'd even entered the café, sitting at one of the stools along the high table lining the window. A few people were on their computers or had headphones on, but Mia was simply sipping coffee staring out the window.

Keeping an eye on the woman, Reese got in line and ordered a drink, hoping she'd make Mia more comfortable when she approached her.

A few minutes later, latte in hand, she moved in next to the empty seat. "Mia? I'm Rachel..."

The woman looked almost startled but nodded, her gaze sweeping over Reese quickly. Whatever she saw had her expression turning wry. "Even if your hair is a little darker, he really does have a type," she murmured, sadness in her voice as she motioned for Reese to sit.

"Thank you for meeting with me. I...was surprised you answered." Reese didn't have to fake her awkwardness—meeting like this was weird. Even if she was used to going undercover on occasion, sometimes it didn't feel natural. Like now, when approaching a single mom who wasn't a target, but had likely been a victim or at least taken advantage of by an older, more powerful man.

Mia gave a half smile. "I've always been curious and...whatever, your email intrigued me. So, what do you want to know?"

Oh, so they were just getting right down to it. "I've overheard some talk from some of the others at the wellness center and...god, I feel so stupid. I thought

I was the only one." Reese rolled her eyes at herself, hoping she came across as sympathetic. "But when Ben offered me a severance and said I had to sign an NDA it felt...well, as if he'd done it before. Then I overheard some of the others talking and..." She cleared her throat, wishing Mia would say *something*. "Anyway, I, uh, I asked around and your name came up." There, that left it vague enough and would hopefully encourage the woman to talk.

Mia took a sip of her coffee, looked out the slightly fogged window at passing traffic. It was warm enough in the café, but not enough to take off their coats. Outside, people chatted with each other as they strolled past, everyone lost in their own worlds. And Mia was lost in the one in her head.

Finally she turned back to Reese. "I thought I was the only one too." Her expression was dry, cynical, and so unlike the smiling woman in the few photos she'd found online. She'd looked younger, freer in some of the ones Reese had scoured from friends' social media accounts. "He's really, really good at making you feel special. But...I'm not and neither are you. Not to him anyway," she added, slightly wincing. "I don't mean that as a dig or anything. He is who he is and he's not changing. I would have stayed too, which is pathetic but..." Shaking her head, she looked back out the window.

"I'm so angry," Reese said, leaning into her role. "He's using his position to basically...I don't know..." She pretended to scramble for the right words when in reality she wanted to shred Ben Kingston for using his position of power to charm women into his bed and then discard them when he was done.

"Use women until we're no longer what he wants?" Mia supplied, her voice tired. "Look, if he offered you a severance, take it. If you don't, what's the alternative? To take him to court? No one there will testify against him and the sheriff is in his pocket. He's got powerful friends, Rachel. Be smart and don't make an enemy of him. His pockets run deep and..." She sighed, shook her head. "Just be smart."

"Did he ever hurt you?" she asked quietly, hoping this was the opening she'd been waiting for. Maybe that was what had happened with Aubry Boyle. Maybe she'd pushed back, wanted him to leave his wife, and things had spiraled out of control.

Mia blinked in surprise, however. "Ah, if you mean, physically, *no*." She laughed lightly, as if the idea was beyond ridiculous. "But he will *never* leave his wife. He doesn't love her, and I'm pretty sure she only tolerates him, but they make a lot of money. And no, he never hurt me. He…"

Trailing off, she looked as if she wanted to say more, but ended up sliding off her stool instead, to-go cup in her gloved hand.

"Look. I probably shouldn't have agreed to meet up, but I remember how wrecked I was when things ended between us. I was hoping I could spare you some heartache. If you think by refusing to sign a severance or whatever, it will make a difference, it won't. He's a man-child, something it took me a while to actually understand. He's never going to change, *never* going to leave his wife. And she's the one who runs that place, in case you haven't realized that. He'll *never* leave her…and he really does have powerful friends. If he's offering you something, take it and run. And never, ever look back. Make a home somewhere else and live your best life." Mia gave her a small smile then, a real one, that was likely meant to be encouraging, before she headed out of the café in long, confident strides.

"Should I follow her?" Cash's voice sounded in her earpiece.

"Nah. I don't think we'll get anything out of her."

"Did you notice that she never said Ben's name?" Cash asked.

"Yeah, I caught that too," Reese murmured as she stepped out onto the sidewalk and headed in the opposite direction of Mia. "I cloned her phone just in case, but I don't think we'll get anything from her. She seemed…I don't know, definitely disgusted with him, but just *done* with him."

"Agreed. And since she never once said his name, if for some reason he tried to use this conversation against her, it shouldn't mess with any NDA she signed."

"Those things are oftentimes useless anyway," Reese said. "Especially for a man who doesn't want anyone to know about his affairs." Reese pulled her earpiece out as she slid into the passenger seat.

Cash started the engine and reversed out of his parking spot. "And a man like Ben Kingston only uses them as a flimsy shield. Something the women he convinces to sign them likely don't realize. Because what he fears is anyone finding out about his cheating. He's built this whole empire with his beautiful wife, but it's all fake, based on a lie. So if any of these women spoke out against him, it would destroy the illusion. The NDA wouldn't matter, even if he sued one of them—which I don't think he would. Because once that illusion is gone, everything else would come crumbling down. His wife would likely leave him, or maybe just force him out of the business. The two of them have built their wellness center on the basis of it being a haven for couples. On romance. He'd be in a potentially contentious divorce, not worrying about suing someone. Not to mention the women he's sleeping with are his employees so that's a whole other can of worms." Disgust laced Cash's voice.

"Huh...and what if Aubry Boyle refused to sign an NDA? What if she refused to go quietly? It could be the first time that's ever happened to him. I could see them getting into an argument, her telling him that she won't be silenced, that she's going to tell his wife." Reese tapped her bottom lip. "It could have happened so quickly too. An argument that just got heated and things went sideways."

Cash was silent as he steered them out of the small mountain town. "It's a solid theory, but we have absolutely no evidence," he finally muttered.

"And it's only a theory." Reese pulled up her laptop as he drove. "It could have nothing to do with him. It could be his wife. Adalyn managed to clone Mila's phone and texted me that she's currently running through all her texts."

"Anything good?"

Reese shook her head as she set her phone back down. "No, just work stuff. All business, all the time...and that itself is interesting. Adalyn said that she and her husband literally only text each other about work stuff. No cute emojis, no sweet messages, nothing. Jeez," she muttered, looking at some of them before pulling up another screen. Adalyn was taking care of that so she could focus on other things. "They don't even use fun punctuation. They're like business partners only."

"Maybe it's just the way they communicate."

"True. But the messages are just so businesslike. I don't even text with you like that and we're coworkers."

"Just coworkers, huh?"

"You know what I mean."

"No, I don't know what you mean." Cash's tone was even and she realized she'd walked into a trap.

She cleared her throat, trying to figure out what the hell to say. They were coworkers who'd enjoyed some fun naked time together, that was all. But she couldn't say that aloud. Just like she couldn't say that she continuously fantasized about him, wondered if they could hook up again. Because, again, they worked together. It would simply be foolish.

If a whole lot of fun. *So. Much. Fun.*

Her phone buzzed with an incoming text, saving her from having to respond. But... "Hell. Adalyn says the cops are there. Hurry."

## Chapter 16

Adalyn tried to keep her gait casual as she and Rowan headed down to the main gathering area with the fire pit and outdoor bar area. Before this job she'd worked in dangerous countries, almost all war-torn and some run by dictators. She'd always been undercover-ish, but the actual people she'd worked with had known she worked for the government.

Acting as one part of a not-so-happy-couple was odd in itself, but especially in the bougie setting. She loved camping and hiking, but she did that in tents or in a camper—this wellness retreat was something for rich people. What she was pretending to be.

When Rowan took her hand in his gloved one, she had to actively not jump out of her skin from surprise. At the moment, her respect for deep-cover spies had jumped exponentially. And it had already been incredibly high.

"I only saw one cop car," she murmured to Rowan as they strode into the gathering area.

A few other couples were sitting around the fire pit, talking and enjoying the warmth of the fire, and the bartender was still working, so maybe the cop car meant nothing? But she'd seen the flashing lights from the window in the bedroom and her mind had gone to the worst-case scenario—that they'd found Aubry Boyle.

He squeezed her hand once and they strode up to the outdoor bar. Even though it was mid-afternoon, the Edison-style lights were on above them.

"Hot chocolate, s'mores or something stronger? Or all of the above?" The woman behind the bar had on a white puffy jacket, white ski pants and her blonde hair was pulled up in a high ponytail. If there'd been any slopes on the property, she looked ready for them.

"Coffee for me," Rowan murmured. "And my wife would like a hot chocolate, extra marshmallows and whipped cream."

Oh, so he was ordering for her? She knew he was doing it to get under her skin, but whatever. That drink was exactly what she'd wanted so screw him. She kept a smile in place as she leaned forward. "I saw a police car earlier, is everything okay?"

The woman blinked, her eyes widening for a moment before she shook her head, as if shaking off the notion that anything could be wrong. "Oh yeah. I think one of the horses got out or something and they were worried one of them got stolen." She waved a hand in the air as if that made sense.

When in reality, it was the dumbest thing Adalyn had heard all week. When the woman turned her back to them, Adalyn shot Rowan a sideways glance. He simply lifted a skeptical brow. No one called the cops if their horse got out, especially not in a place like Montana.

But fine, she'd play along. "We had plans to ride in an hour. Do you think we should postpone?"

"Oh...ah, I don't really know. But one of the guides is going to be taking out a few couples on four-wheelers in about half an hour. You should definitely sign up for it. It's a lot of fun. You'll get to go sledding at the top of one of the hills and they'll pull you back up on the four-wheeler if you don't want to walk or ride." She kept talking as she made their drinks.

That actually sounded fun, but they weren't here to have fun. They were here for a job. "Thanks for the recommendation," she said, however, keeping an easy smile on her face.

As they walked away, Adalyn glanced at Rowan. "Want to head to the stables?"

He nodded, his breath coming out in white puffs, mixing with the wispy steam from his coffee.

She slid her earpiece in and called Elijah. "How are things on your end?"

"Gage and I are good. We've roped in a few others to comb through the cloned phones and I'm keeping an eye on the surveillance cameras. Did you find out anything about the cops yet?"

"No, we're headed in that direction now, going to see what we can dig up."

"Good. I checked out the local police feed and couldn't find any call that came in directly to dispatch from the wellness center. Or even in the last hour at all."

"Huh. That's weird."

"Maybe, but it's a small town. Someone could have reached out directly to a cop they know or the sheriff or whoever."

"True. We'll keep you posted."

"I'm running the phone records of all the cops on the force right now," Elijah said.

Adalyn paused, still getting used to how quickly Elijah, Gage, Reese and a few others could handle things. "Sounds good, thanks."

She was good with tech stuff for the most part, but they were on a different level. But it was weird to be in a civilian setting and technically—okay, no technical about it—breaking the law on the regular. She'd done a lot of shady shit when she'd been with the CIA. And gotten fired for it. Well, they'd let her resign, but everyone knew she'd been on the verge of being fired if she hadn't resigned. And if they'd been able to prove what she'd done, they'd have likely pulled her up on charges of...a whole lot of things. Well screw them. She had zero regrets. If they tried to come after her later, she'd deal with it or disappear.

Taking this job with Skye and her crew had been another middle finger to her former life. At least now she wasn't restricted by red tape. Not that she'd always been restricted. But now she was working with people she respected, actually liked. And she wanted to make a difference, to feel like she was helping people instead of being a cog in a dicked-up machine.

The walkway to the stables was paved and had been cleared of snow, making it easy to get there.

"So how do you want to handle this?" Rowan asked, his tone all polite and even, nothing like when he'd first found out they'd be working together.

She was surprised he was asking her opinion. "I was thinking we lean into our role, just act like rich, clueless assholes. Or maybe not assholes, but demanding information."

He nodded, his eyes covered by his sunglasses and she was glad for it. She didn't want to see his eyes, didn't want to look at him at all, if she was being honest. Because being near him just reminded her of how badly she'd screwed up. She'd trusted the wrong person and innocent people had paid the price.

Doing what she always did—compartmentalizing her monumental life screwups—she leaned into her cover as a wealthy heiress to some textile company no one had ever heard of, but that had websites and enough references so that the people here would believe she was who she said she was. Not that Adalyn thought they looked too deeply into who stayed here as long as their clients paid.

"Lights are off now," she murmured to Rowan, stating the obvious as they approached the idling F-250 with *Sheriff's Department* in blue on the side.

Walking into the stable like they owned the place, Adalyn took Rowan's hand in hers as they approached a woman in dark jeans, boots, a thick jacket with the sheriff's department logo on it, as well as a ball cap covering her long, dark braid. Detective, maybe. She was alone, her cell phone in hand. The woman looked as if she was about to kick them out so Adalyn smiled big.

She could tell from the woman's scowl that being an asshole wasn't going to get her anywhere so she decided to go with the sweet-and-friendly approach. "Hi, we've got an appointment to go riding soon but saw your truck out there. And someone said a horse was stolen. Is this a bad time? Is everything okay with the horse?"

The woman blinked, but before she could answer, Mila Kingston strode out of one of the stables, a big smile on her pretty face. "Oh, Mr. and Mrs. Milsap, how lovely to see you."

Adalyn smiled right back. "Mrs. Kingston—"

"Oh, just call me Mila, please. I overheard you, and to answer you, all our horses are fine. Everything is fine, wonderful even. Someone called by mistake but everything is running like a well-oiled machine. I know you two are signed up to ride, so if you're ready now, I can get the horses prepared and take you out myself."

Adalyn could see that the woman—detective?—wanted to argue, but surprisingly didn't say anything.

The woman shoved her phone into her jacket pocket, her mouth pulling into a thin line.

"Well if you're sure…" Adalyn looked at the other woman, kept her smile in place. "I'm sorry for barging in here demanding answers. My brother-in-law is in law enforcement and I know better, but my curiosity got the better of me. I'm Ava, by the way. And you're Officer Lippman?" she said, reading the name sewn into the jacket pocket.

"Ah, Detective Lippman. Valerie," she added, thawing a fraction. But she frowned as she looked at Mila Kingston, clearly upset or maybe just annoyed about something. "I'll be heading out," was all she said before she stalked out of the stables.

"I thought Wayne was going to be taking us riding," Rowan said, his tone casual as he strolled over to one of the stables and gently petted one of the horses.

A big gray and white horse with intelligent eyes whinnied softly as he petted her.

Despite her desire to remain unmoved by her arrogant, obnoxious *coworker*, she found herself smiling at Rowan, then told herself it was only part of her cover. She was supposed to be his wife, after all.

"You're a good girl," he murmured to the horse, pressing his face against her nose, which the horse seemed to absolutely love.

"She's the best girl and that's who you'll be riding," Mila said, smiling at both of them. "Her name's Lady and she's an Andalusian. She prefers men and I think it's clear that she likes you, so great choice."

But something about her smile was off. It had that "shopkeeper" look to it or maybe it would be called her "customer service" smile. Whatever, she had stress lines bracketing her mouth and was definitely trying to cover it. She also hadn't said why Wayne wasn't going to be taking them riding, which was interesting. Adalyn wasn't going to push either. No, she was going to take advantage of this ride and try to information-gather as best she could. Not that she expected Mila to tell her that she'd killed her husband's mistress, but people often dropped information without even realizing it.

"I'm a novice so hopefully you'll put me with a friendly one," Adalyn said on a laugh.

"Oh, you'll be riding Cookie. I saw the questionnaire so I know you're a beginner. And with the snow and impending storm, we won't be going too far anyway. But I need to get my girls out, and of all my horses, they love the snow."

"Sounds good." Though it didn't at all. She loved looking at horses, but riding them was another matter entirely. Fast rope out of a helicopter? No problem. Rappel down the side of a building. Yep, done it. Chase down bad guys in enemy territory? Sure, and got the bullet wound to prove it.

But ride a giant beast that could decide it doesn't like her smell or whatever, then decide to throw her off on a whim... Horses and animals in general terrified her. Well, except cats. Cats, she understood.

It didn't take long for Mila to get them geared up and ready to go, trotting gently down the trail.

"I'm surprised more people aren't out here," Adalyn said as her horse decided to shimmy up next to Mila's.

Rowan's horse was slowly strutting her stuff, her tail swishing adorably as he pulled up the rear.

"In the spring and winter, I can't keep our guests out of the stables. But usually in the winter, people like to unwind in the spa, meditating or on four-wheelers. So I'm happy you two wanted to get out. What do you think of our great state so far?"

"I think beautiful doesn't do it justice," Adalyn said, laughing. "I feel like we walked into a postcard. A really terrifying one where I know bears and other things are lurking nearby."

Her words made the other woman chuckle, very clearly at ease on her big horse. Just like Rowan was—he looked far too comfortable, all rugged and annoyingly handsome on Lady. Meanwhile, Adalyn was clutching onto the reins for dear life, worried that at any moment she was going to get tossed and break her neck. *Ugh.* It would figure if a horse killed her.

"Well, we do have a lot of wildlife around here, but we patrol our property regularly and the horse paths are safe, so no worries at all."

"That's good to know. So how long have you and your husband owned this place exactly? I know it's on the website but I've forgotten already."

Mila's jaw tightened ever so slightly at the mention of her husband, but smiled all the same. "About ten years. And this resort is a labor of love."

"Well it shows. I can tell how much you've put into it."

"It's my life." There was a note in her voice that Adalyn couldn't quite pinpoint. Wistfulness, maybe? But definitely truth. This place was the woman's life, and if someone had come along and threatened to upend it…there was no telling how Mila might have reacted.

Because almost all people could react in violence depending on the right, or wrong, circumstances. It was those split-second choices that could change your life forever, for better or worse.

They fell into a friendly conversation as they rode along the snow-dusted path, with tall ponderosa pine trees on either side of them, also covered in a pretty white higher up in the branches, with bits of green peeking out.

During a lull, Adalyn shot off a text to Reese that the cops showing up didn't appear to be anything. But they needed to look into it—needed to find out who had called the detective and why. A detective hadn't arrived for a friendly visit or a missing horse. Someone had called for a reason, and with what they knew about Aubry Boyle, and the sheriff's refusal to treat her as a missing person, maybe it was tied together.

Or maybe not. But Adalyn planned to get to the bottom of things and to find the missing girl. Who, experience told her, was likely already dead. Another picture had popped up on the girl's social media feed this morning, another one of falling snow and some cheesy caption.

And the picture was recent, according to Elijah. So someone had her phone. And maybe it actually was Aubry and she'd just gone off-grid, but she hadn't accessed her bank account, hadn't used her credit card, and hadn't paid one of her recent bills. Which, according to her history of on-time payments, was out of the ordinary.

Something had happened here. They just needed to figure out what it was.

At a sudden whinny behind them, Adalyn turned. "Oh shit!" she barked before she could stop herself. Because a huge-ass...mountain lion? Cougar? Oh god...a large feline was standing in the pathway behind them, staring straight at Rowan.

"Be calm and no sudden movements." Mila moved up behind her, on foot, Adalyn saw out of the corner of her eyes.

*Sure, be calm, not a problem.* Cookie whinnied nervously underneath Adalyn, stomping her legs in annoyance—or maybe fear. Adalyn could relate.

Rowan was still as well, keeping his gaze on the cat as Mila moved up next to them, lifted her handgun.

*Oh...no!* Adalyn wanted to tell her not to shoot the cat, but then the woman aimed to the side, too far to hit it, and fired.

"Get out of here!" Mila shouted as the sound of her gunshot echoed through the mountains.

It was like the starter at a race because Adalyn's horse reared back and took off into the brush.

"No, stop!" Adalyn leaned forward, holding on for dear life as her horse raced through the snow, kicking it up as Cookie raced through the thick stand of trees at full speed.

"Oh, Mrs. Milsap! It's too dangerous to go off trail...damn it." Mila's voice trailed off but she heard Rowan calling out and the beat of his horse's hooves nearby.

"Sit up and pull on the reins. Use a calming, strong voice!" he called out.

*Sure, easy freaking peasy.* Her heart was an erratic beat in her chest, thundering as loudly as the damn horses as she ducked to avoid being hit with a low-lying branch.

"Stop...ah, halt! It's time for you to stop, Cookie. Right now!" Adalyn sat up slightly, tugged on the reins, but Cookie shook her head, whinnied loudly before she jumped over a fallen log.

"Halt!" Rowan's strong voice called out a moment before Mila flew past her, riding her horse like a boss. The other woman moved her horse in front of Adalyn and Cookie and called out another order.

Cookie slowed, pranced, then stuck her nose up in the air as she fully stopped. She tossed her mane a few times but seemed content to stay calm.

Adalyn's heart, however, was anything but. "Is the cat...mountain lion, okay?"

"Yeah, it ran off." Mila shook her head, a frown tugging at her mouth. "Shouldn't have even been out here. I know where her den is and she's too far from it. We're okay though and we're just going to head back... No, Mr. Milsap, we're not getting off the horses out here. I need to get you guys back on the trail..."

That was when Adalyn saw that Rowan had dismounted and was stalking across the snow looking like a rugged cowboy himself.

Rowan ignored her as he loosely slung the reins of Lady over a branch of a pine sapling, then trudged through the thick snow, his boots making crunching sounds. "I see something," he murmured, the only explanation he was apparently giving either of them.

Sighing, Mila slid off her horse with ease and stalked after him with determined strides.

Adalyn might not like the man very much, but he was still her partner, so if he said he saw something, it was likely worth checking out. She slid off her horse—and fell in the snow with an ungraceful thud. Luckily Cookie didn't decide to stomp her to death.

No, her horse just looked down at her as if she was stupid. Which felt about right. She did as Rowan had, then looped her reins on the branch with his horse.

"Mr. Milsap, we don't have time..." Mila's voice trailed off as Adalyn reached them and Adalyn could see why.

Rowan was crouched down, brushing away snow to reveal... *Oh god.* The sleeve and arm of someone. A woman. A gold bracelet glinted on her wrist, twinkling under the afternoon sun peeking through the trees. He kept digging through the snow and Adalyn knelt down next to him. She wasn't sure if this would make sense for her cover, but whatever. She wasn't going to let him do this alone.

Moving around him, she started scooping up snow with her glove-covered hands, tossing it to the side until... A blue-tinged face appeared, eyes wide open and glazed over in death, and what looked like handprints around her throat.

Aubry Boyle.

"You need to call that detective," Rowan said, sadness in his voice as he stood, then took a step back.

She did the same. They needed to preserve the scene.

Mila stood there, however, staring in shock down at the body. "Oh my god, that's...Aubry. She worked here, went home weeks ago. Or...I thought she did." Covering her mouth, she looked as if she was going to be sick.

"No!" Rowan snapped out, his voice hard, making both of them stare at him.

Blinking, Mila focused on him.

"Don't get sick here. This is a crime scene. Even if she wasn't killed here, she was dumped here. We need to preserve this as much as possible so we're going to take our horses back to the path, then you're going to call the police. Or I can. But we need to get someone out here immediately."

"Of course, of course." Mila seemed to snap out of it as she hurried back to her horse, grabbed her phone from her saddlebag.

"Here," Rowan murmured, helping Adalyn get back onto her horse.

She wished she didn't need his help, but she took it and slid back on the beast as Mila's quiet voice filled the air.

"We've found a body."

# Chapter 17

"I knew it was coming," Reese murmured as they sprinted through the woods, only slowing as they reached the upcoming trail that would lead them back to the wellness ranch. They'd stashed the truck back in its hiding spot and now they needed to make it back before anyone realized they were missing. "Or I thought so, but…I was still holding out hope that she was alive."

"Me too." Cash's expression was grim as they reached the trail.

They slowed but kept up a brisk pace as they walked. At this point they had to pretend that they had no idea what was going on.

"So what happens now? We were hired to find her and…" Cash stalked onward, but took slower strides to keep pace with her, she noticed.

Reese moved fast, but she was still a bit shorter than him and she appreciated that he was adjusting for her. "I'm not totally sure, but I can guess. In the past we've only had this issue once when looking for a missing person, but it was a different kind of situation. I think we should stay and keep investigating even though the police are now involved. It might not be a missing persons case for us now, but the police didn't do their job before—and maybe understandably so, given that it looked like she'd left on her own. I can't say. But I want to stay and see what else we can find. Especially since Mia Williams made it clear that Ben Kingston is tight with local law enforcement."

Cash shoved out a sigh. "I'm glad we're staying. I want to find out who did this. Have you heard anything else from the others?"

"No texts after the last one. Okay, here we go," she whispered as they reached the end of the trail. There was no one around, but still. She slid her hand in his as they walked along the paved path. She could have told herself it was as part of their cover, but she'd be lying to herself.

When they reached the main road where the majority of the cabins were, a college-aged man driving an ATV stopped in front of them. "Hey, we're gathering everyone up for a meeting. I've been going around to the different cabins for those who didn't answer calls."

"Oh..." Cash trailed off in confusion. "Yeah, we went out on another hike. Is everything okay?"

"I'll give you a ride," the guy said instead of actually answering.

"Ah, sure." Cash shrugged as he helped Reese into the back seat, then slid in with her and wrapped an arm around her shoulders. Cold seeped through her so she leaned into him, inwardly cursing herself.

She knew that once Aubry went missing, once Joelle saw someone removing all of the woman's things from her cabin, and then the fake posts online, that finding Aubry alive had been a pipe dream. Even so, she'd held on to that little kernel of hope that they'd be able to find her, save her. Reese wanted to at least find out who the hell had killed her and give her and her family justice.

The ATV stopped right where the outdoor bar and fire pit gathering area was, and sure enough, there was a cluster of people sitting around the fire.

"Thanks for the ride," Cash murmured, not missing a beat as he took Reese's hand in his.

Her boots crunched over a pile of snow that hadn't been cleared as they headed toward the circular seating area. Instinctively she looked for Adalyn and Rowan, but didn't see them.

Cash stiffened next to her and that was when she saw where his gaze was.

On his ex.

Isabella Vance.

*What the hell?* The woman was sitting on a small bench in front of the fire pit instead of one of the Adirondack-style chairs, cuddled up with a ridiculously handsome man who had his arm around her. Her fiancé.

"Did you know she was going to be here?" Reese murmured as they moved toward two free seats.

"Nope." His jaw ticked once.

"It's weird that she just showed up." Reese kept her expression neutral, casual as they sat on a stone bench with cushions to save their butts from the ice cold.

"I agree."

"Well try to look less pissed. Or do something with your face. We're supposed to be confused," she whispered, but stopped talking as one of the women she recognized from the bus, Rae, sat next to them. Her eyes were a little puffy, as if she'd been crying. Ah, she was with the cheater, per Adalyn.

"Do you know what's going on?" Rae asked as she held her hands out to the fire in front of them, sans husband, Reese couldn't help but notice.

"No, some guy just picked us up when we were coming back from a hike, called us here." Reese glanced over at Isabella, unable to stop herself.

The redhead was in all white and looked...ugh, fabulous. Like she'd stepped off the cover of some skiing or outdoor magazine. Probably called *Supermodels Who Ski and Marry Men Who Look Like Kennedys.*

Gah! *Get out of your head*, she ordered herself. And failed.

And the tall, elegant woman was staring at Cash, calculation in her dark gaze. Oooh, Reese did not like this woman, didn't like the way she made her feel insecure just for existing.

Reese knew she was being stupid, was letting herself get caught up in feelings that had nothing to do with the here and now and everything to do with her boarding school days. She hadn't fit in then, hadn't even tried to because she'd been so worried she'd try and fail. Eventually she'd found her people, but the first year had been rough.

And women—girls, then—who'd looked just like Isabella had made her feel two inches tall. Some intentionally, some not, and she knew that nothing about today had anything to do with her high school days. But something about this woman brought up her insecurities.

And she didn't need her therapist to tell her what that was.

The woman had been with Cash, was looking at him right now as if she was imagining him naked. Jealousy she hadn't even known she was capable of surged inside her. She tried to squash the feeling because holy shit, now was *not* the time or place. They were still on a job and Cash wasn't hers.

Taking a deep breath, she turned to look at Cash and found him watching her, not Isabella. She blinked up at him and forgot to breathe. The intensity in his eyes, the raw hunger, stripped her down to her barest self. It was as if he saw the real her, right down to her most neurotic side and that scared her.

He opened his mouth to say something, but she'd never know what that was because Mila Kingston suddenly called out, breaking through whatever haze that had been.

"Thank you all for gathering. I'm sure some of you have seen the police presence and we have a sad announcement. Someone who used to work here was recently found…passed away on our property."

That was a weird way to say *murdered*.

Mila cleared her throat as she continued, her husband standing behind her, his hands clasped in front of him, his head bowed. *Out of guilt*, Reese wondered?

"We're not sure what happened but the police are working to find out. The police believe this happened weeks ago but everyone here will need to answer a few questions. We understand that this is a terrible thing and we're offering full refunds to everyone. And for anyone who wants to leave after talking to one of the detectives, we also understand…"

Reese glanced around at the employees' faces as Mila continued talking, offering an on-site therapist to speak to, which felt over-the-top considering no one here had known her or had found the body. Or even seen the body, as far as Reese knew. But it was clear they were offering it to their employees as well, which made sense—and Reese didn't see Joelle anywhere, made a mental note to text her as soon as they wrapped up.

Which thankfully didn't take long. As Mila finished speaking, some of the couples drifted off, but others stayed and murmured to each other.

"Are you going to stay?" Reese asked Rae, who hadn't made a move to leave her spot.

"I honestly don't know. Maybe? I don't know anything anymore," she murmured more to herself than Reese.

And in that moment Reese wanted to pull the stranger into a hug. She didn't think Rae needed a week getaway with her cheating husband, she needed a good divorce attorney.

The woman stood, smiled sadly at them, before she left the group.

"Ten o'clock," Cash murmured, gently squeezing her hand.

Frowning, since it was afternoon, she turned to look at him and realized that he meant Isabella was homing in on them at their ten o'clock, practically dragging her fiancé along.

*Great. Juuuust great.*

Reese stood with Cash, glided right into his side where she fit perfectly, thank you very much, and slid an arm around him. She couldn't start humping him to stake her claim, right? Or just start making out? Definitely not.

"Surprised seeing you here." Isabella's smile was wide, her expression guileless, but Reese knew what she'd seen earlier. Had witnessed that calculation. "Cash, I believe you know John Danforth?"

Cash nodded politely at the other man, shook his hand briefly. "So what are you two doing here? They seemed to have a pretty strict policy about only showing up on Sundays."

John laughed lightly. "My family is friends with Ben's so they made an exception."

"We got lucky—or maybe not, now—that they had an opening this week and didn't mind us coming a day late. We've been so busy with wedding planning and both our schedules opened up, so…" She lifted her shoulder.

"John, Isabella, this is Reese, my fiancée," Cash said when the woman didn't continue.

Isabella blinked in true surprise, looking like a deer caught in headlights, but John held out his hand to her. "Congratulations. I think I might know your parents? Ah, Reese Sinclair, right?"

"That's right," she said, smiling politely as she took his hand. She didn't know too much about the man—but she had been curious enough to look him up since she'd known he was engaged to Cash's ex. The man lived on a very nice trust fund, but he did at least donate to worthy causes. From what she'd gathered, he partied hard with his college buddies, occasionally showed up to the office of the company his father owned—and was supposedly going to take over one day.

"Oh right, your mother is wonderful," Isabella added, her eyes narrowing slightly. "You're in cybersecurity or something right?"

"Or something." She smiled back, keeping her polite smile firmly in place.

"Well we're going to get out of here," Cash interjected smoothly, stepping back ever so slightly, his grip firm around Reese. "It's been a long day, but maybe we'll see you later."

"Of course." John's tone was casual and friendly, but Isabella couldn't mask her annoyance.

Which made Reese smile just a bit wider. She leaned into Cash as they strode away, moving through the murmuring guests—everyone was asking questions that had no answers.

She slid her earpiece in and called Rowan once they were far enough away. "Where are you?" she asked the moment he answered.

"Just talked to the cops, almost back to our cabin."

"We'll meet you there." She disconnected and managed not to look over her shoulder to see if Cash's ex was heading in their direction. "So did you tell her that you were going to be here this week?" Reese tried to keep her tone casual, wasn't sure if she failed.

"Who…Isabella?" Cash snorted, kicked a clump of snow out of his way as they headed up the steps to Adalyn and Rowan's cabin.

"That's not an answer." It was more of a deflection.

"No, I didn't invite her," he practically snarled, dropping his arm around her.

Which was just fine with her. "Maybe it came up in conversation and you accidentally told her. We just have to be careful about stuff like that," she murmured, glancing at the street behind them as she knocked on the front door.

Two couples were headed to their cabins.

The door swung open but Cash was definitely not done, given his angry stalk into the cabin behind her. "I didn't say anything to anyone." His voice was even more heated as he slid his boots off.

She did the same, nodding at Adalyn, who was looking between them with wide eyes.

"Okay, fine, if you say you didn't, then you didn't. I saw that she texted you the other day—I was not looking. It just popped up when we were at the airport and you told me to text Hailey back for you. I didn't read the whole message or anything."

"Yeah she texted me and I ignored it. I never respond to her. Or...rarely."

"Okay." Reese lifted a shoulder, considering the matter closed.

"I feel like you're humoring me, like you don't really believe me."

Adalyn was slowly moving away from the foyer, clearly not wanting any part of this.

And Reese didn't want any part of this either, was regretting asking him at all. "You could barely look at the woman at that gala, yet she still texts you and you haven't...*blocked* her? I block my dumbass exes."

"Fine, I'll block her right now." He whipped out his phone.

"Oh please, I don't care what you do! I was simply asking if you'd told her because I thought it was weird that she showed up. I don't want to argue." She turned away from him, wondering how the hell things had spiraled so quickly.

She could feel him behind her—and hear him grumbling—as she headed into the open living room to find both Rowan and Adalyn sitting on different couches.

Reese sat on one of the single chairs by the fireplace that faced them. Cash chose to stand by the fireplace, arms crossed over his chest as he vibrated with annoyance.

"Everything okay?" Rowan looked between the two of them cautiously.

"Yep, great. So what happened out there? How'd you find her? Did you see anything that might help us?"

"We had a bit of a scare with a mountain lion and ended up off trail. I saw a glint of something in the snow…" Rowan shook his head, his expression grim. "She had on a gold bracelet and it caught the sun just right. I didn't know what it was, but I knew it didn't belong out in the wild. She was…" Rowan shook his head, his expression grim. "She was mostly covered in snow and she'd been strangled. There was definitive bruising around her throat. Looked like hands. I have no idea if she was assaulted otherwise, but it was murder."

"Yeah," Adalyn murmured quietly.

"You were with Mila Kingston at the time?"

"Yeah and she looked truly surprised. She could have been faking, or maybe it was simply the shock of seeing the body. I don't know." Adalyn shook her head.

"She was almost sick," Rowan added. "But, yeah, she could have been faking."

"What does your gut say?"

He was silent for a long moment. "I don't know. I'm leaning toward believing her surprise, but that could have been because she hid the body and Aubry was found at all. So what's the plan?"

Reese glanced at Cash, who was still annoyed with her, given his body language, but he lifted a shoulder.

"I'll need to confirm with Skye but I want to stay. I want to find out who the hell killed Aubry Boyle."

"Me too," Adalyn said even as Rowan nodded.

Reese's phone buzzed before she could respond, and when she saw Elijah's name on the screen she answered. "Hey, you're on speaker."

"I found something interesting. I think Mila Kingston is having an affair. With Detective Valerie Lippman."

## Chapter 18

His earlier annoyance at Reese's questioning somewhat dimmed, Cash sat next to her on the couch. "Why do you think they're having an affair?" he asked Elijah.

"Phone records. And the reason we didn't notice this before is because we only looked at the Kingstons' phones. I looked into Lippman's phone records and she consistently calls and texts with another number. A burner phone which was bought with Mila Kingston's credit card." He muttered something about how if you're going to be sneaky that you needed to commit, to not half-ass it.

"How many calls and texts?" Reese asked.

"Thousands. They text every day, all throughout the day. And I remembered that Joelle told you that Mila Kingston disappears every Wednesday for a doctor's appointment. Their phones—the burner, Lippman's and Mila's—all hit the same tower around that time. Not that that's definitive proof of anything, but their phones are also silent for a couple hours on Wednesdays. No texting, calling, et cetera."

"If she's using a burner, it would explain why you didn't find anything when you cloned her phone," Cash murmured to Reese.

Frowning, she bit her bottom lip as she stared at her phone. Finally she said. "Okay, thanks. I'm not sure what we're going to do with this, but it's really good. Have you seen anything on the surveillance cameras?"

"Nothing usable. I haven't been able to see Mila and Ben in the same room. I'm hoping to get them on camera, maybe admit something, but nothing that ties into this yet." He was silent for a moment, then said. "At least Aubry's mom will be able to bury her daughter. It's not a great outcome, but I'm guessing she was dead before you guys got there—before Joelle even contacted us. There's nothing you could have done."

"Yeah, I know," Reese murmured, still frowning. "I'll call you if we need anything. Thanks for this."

As she ended the call, she sighed and leaned back on the couch.

"Where do we go from here?" Cash asked. When he'd been in the army, he'd been told what doors to break down and done it. Or what enemy combatants to target, and done it. Being involved in an investigation was a lot different and the parameters of this one had just changed.

Or shifted, really.

Reese scrubbed a hand over her face. "I don't know yet. Let's head back to our cabin and wait for the cops to talk to us. How were they with you guys?" She looked between the other two.

"They barely talked to us. Detective Lippman and another detective. Ah, Frank Conroy, they were the two who showed up," Rowan said. "They just took our names and wanted to know what happened, compare it to Mila Kingston's story I guess."

"Did Detective Lippman take her statement?" Cash asked.

"Nope." Adalyn shook her head. "I didn't think about it at the time, but they didn't interact much. Lippman took my statement and cordoned off the body, but Conroy took Rowan's and Mila's. It was all professional."

Reese stood. "Okay, then...we're going to head back to our cabin in case the detectives stop by. I think it seems normal to do that in a situation right now."

Adalyn nodded. "Is any of your equipment out or anything?"

"Just my laptop but it's protected so I'm not worried. Everything else is in my suitcase locked up. And I doubt they'll ask to search our belongings."

Cash headed out with Reese, still feeling out of sorts from earlier. As they reached the bottom of the short set of stairs, their boots touching the dusting of snow on the walkway, Reese paused and turned to him.

"I'm sorry about earlier. I was being a jerk. But that's on me, not you. I hate losing anyone," she murmured even as she turned from him.

He fell in step with her and automatically wrapped his arm around her shoulders, wanting to comfort her. And himself, if he was being honest. Not because they were undercover, but because he wanted to touch her, to feel anchored. "I didn't tell my ex anything, for the record. I didn't even talk to her. And…maybe I should have blocked her before. I don't know why I haven't." Cash wasn't sure why he was confessing this to Reese.

Okay, lie. He knew why he was. For the first time ever, he felt like he could be himself with a woman. Like the way Hailey and Jesse were with each other. Cash and Reese might have grown up very differently, but she saw him in a way no one else did. And she wasn't impressed by his money or, much to his annoyance, his charm.

Oh, she was attracted to him, no doubt about that. But she called him out on anything she saw fit and it was sexy as hell. He felt out of his depth with her, terrified in a way he liked.

"It's hard to say goodbye to the past, to admit we made a mistake. Or maybe…you're not over her?" Reese's voice was low as they approached their cabin. Instead of using the front door, they used the back since it faced the road.

"Oh, I'm over her." He'd been over Isabella even before things had imploded between them.

"Hmm." Reese didn't say more as she opened the door, stepped inside, immediately scanned for anything out of the ordinary.

Cash wanted to refute that little sound, to deny it, but realized that he would just sound defensive. He wasn't sure why Isabella had shown up, but he didn't like it. Instead of pushing anything with Reese, he decided to search the place.

"I'll do a quick sweep." He headed for the hallway before she could protest, needing some space from her before he opened up more. He scrubbed a hand over his face as he reached the top landing, but then he moved into action, checking for signs that anyone had been in the place. They'd planted small cameras at the front and back entrance as a precaution but he believed in being thorough.

"Cash," Reese called out and he had the distinct image of her calling out his name under much different circumstances.

But he shut that shit down. For now.

He found her in the kitchen, her laptop open, her eyebrows lifted as she took her earbuds out and turned the volume up. She motioned to the screen, which had multiple feeds up. "Elijah texted me, told me to check this out. This happened five minutes ago." She pressed play on one of the feeds, from Mila and Ben Kingston's office.

Ben Kingston was sitting against the front of the messy desk in their office, holding his phone to his ear. "The cops have nothing to do with us. No…" There was a long pause, then, "No. Look, we're still on for the next handoff. Nothing has changed." Another pause. "I don't give a shit what your guy saw. There are just dumbass detectives here because someone died. This has absolutely nothing to do with us."

"Someone?" Cash growled. Ben Kingston was talking about Aubry Boyle like she was no one.

"He also didn't say murdered, which is interesting."

"Can you figure out who he was talking to?"

"Not from here," she muttered.

"Look," Ben said. "We'll meet up at our usual place. Midnight." A pause, then, "I swear they'll be gone by then. Bring what you're supposed to and I'll pay you. Just like always… No! if you involve him, we'll both be sorry…" Ben straightened and she could see the relief in his body language. "That's more like it. I'll see you tonight." He ended the call, then nearly jumped when his wife strode into the office. "Oh, hey."

Her back was to the camera so Reese pulled up the other one, giving them a view of both of them. Cash tried to read her body language, her expression as she stared at her husband. Her jaw was tight.

"You couldn't say anything to our guests?" she finally asked, her voice low. Frustrated.

He turned away from her and started gathering some of the papers on the desk and stacking them. "You had it handled. I didn't want to interrupt."

She nudged him out of the way and stopped his hands. "Leave this alone. I know where everything is." She turned back to face him, her expression hard now. "Were you screwing her? Aubry Boyle?"

Ben's eyes widened. "What? How could you ask me that?"

Mila rolled her eyes. "Oh Jesus, you were. Damn it," she muttered. Then she looked him dead in the face again. "Did you kill her?"

"I can't believe you're asking me that," he snarled, keeping his voice pitched low. Before she could respond, he turned and stalked from the office.

"He definitely didn't answer her question about murder," Cash said.

"No, he did not." Reese looked up at him, her expression thoughtful. "We need to follow him tonight."

"We'll have to do it without making any noise which means ATVs are out."

"We could borrow one of the horses. There are only two cameras at the stables and they're on the outside. I can set them on a loop while we're gone."

"We run the risk of someone finding the horses missing."

She shrugged. "This whole job is a risk."

"True enough. I'm in. Adalyn and Rowan can be our backup. Our eyes and ears here around the wellness center."

Reese nodded, clearly satisfied. "He's into something shady. It kind of sounds like drugs."

"Yeah, and this would be the perfect place for him to transport them. He could move drugs through shipments or...I don't know."

"There are so many ways he could do it. So, I was thinking that we should try to get a tracker on Ben Kingston. That way if we lose him tonight, and chances are we will if we're on horses and trying to remain hidden, we'll still be able to find him."

"What are you thinking?" he asked, his gaze falling to her mouth because he had no control, apparently.

"That you use that famous Cash charm to get close to him, then plant it. He wears the same jacket all the time."

"I can do that. Should I try now or later?"

She looked away from him and he could practically see her brain working overtime. "I say we let the dust settle, let the cops get out of here, then you call him and ask to meet. You're a rich patron, he'll stop by the cabin. Just make it seem like you want reassurances or whatever that we're not in danger, and then shake his hand, do whatever, to get the tracker planted on him. It's really small. If you can get it on his collar or in his pocket, we'll be good."

He nodded, and they paused as there was a hard knock on the back door. Seemed the cops were here.

# Chapter 19

Reese smiled at the bartender as she approached, killing time as she waited for Cash to plant the tracker on Kingston. She'd offered to go with him, but he was going to play the angle that his fiancée—aka her—was scared about the police presence and he wanted to soothe her nerves by talking to one of the owners.

"Something warm with a small kick," she murmured. "Surprise me."

The woman manning the bar tonight grinned. "I know just the thing. How does hot buttered spiced cider sound?"

"Ah, interesting, but I like to try new things so hit me with it." She sat at the bar, enjoying the heat from one of the nearby lamps as she waited.

Out of the corner of her eye, Reese spotted Isabella Vance sans her other half. And by the way the woman was stalking toward her, it was clear she was on a mission to talk to Reese. Or maybe she just really wanted a drink.

"Oh, nice to see you here. Where did Cash get off to?" Isabella's red hair was in a long, luxurious braid draped over her chest, and once again she had on all white. A striking contrast against the woman's bright hair.

"Oh, he's off somewhere." Reese kept her tone even, her smile neutral enough. Though she wasn't sure it could even be considered a smile. Her facial muscles weren't cooperating, and for how she felt at the moment, faking it with some bitch was going to be a stretch.

"I'll have hot tea with lemon." Isabella sat next to her, but thankfully left one stool between them. "So," she continued, turning back to Reese, her eyes bright. "When's the big day?"

"I'm not sure yet. Cash wants to get married as soon as possible, but I want time to plan it."

She laughed lightly. "Oh, I remember, he was the same with me." She paused, her mouth turning into a pout. "Apologies if that's inappropriate."

Reese simply lifted a shoulder, but she was aware of the bartender avidly listening to them even if the woman was pretending not to.

"Well you need to figure out a venue soon because they book up quickly."

She made a noncommittal sound and glanced down at her cell phone, hoping the other woman would take the hint that she wasn't into this conversation. She might not be Cash's real fiancée, but she had a whole lot of feelings for the man. Feelings she was desperately trying not to analyze. Because if she allowed herself to fall down that rabbit hole, it was game over for her sanity.

"We're getting married in four months and I'm already going crazy making sure everything is ready. Not to mention working out like a fiend."

Reese nodded, smiled at her. "Sounds stressful."

"I know it's silly to worry about that before getting married. I think it's great that you're not stressing out about your diet. I wish I could be more like you." There was a slight edge to her tone as she glanced at the high-calorie drink the bartender placed in front of Reese.

Okay so she was just skipping subtlety at this point? Or maybe this *was* Isabella being subtle? Reese didn't think it could be considered passive-aggressive because she'd skated right past passive, but was still not quite aggressive. Hmm, what would that be called? A bitch?

"Thank you," Reese murmured to the bartender, giving her a real smile. Then she turned back to Isabella, looked her dead in her eyes. "You can be like me if you want. It's easy. Just don't cheat on your boyfriends or fiancés. And I'm sure there are going to be more in the future for you, especially when John finds out you're cheating on him just like you cheated on Cash." She gave her a real smile now, one that Hailey called her "eat shit and die" look, before striding away. The cheating thing was a guess, but given the way the woman paled, she'd hit the mark.

Isabella let out a small gasp, but didn't say another word as Reese went to sit closer to the fire pit. Because she wasn't going to run off. Nope, she was going to stay here and wait for Cash.

Out of the corner of her eye she watched as Isabella snatched up her tea, sloshing it over the rim before stalking off, her boots making thudding sounds as she hurried away.

Reese snickered into her drink—which was amazing. She made a note to look up a recipe later even as she watched Rae and Bode approach the fire pit.

They didn't move together as a couple should. He sort of stumbled into his seat, not paying attention to anyone or anything as he plopped down, drink in hand. Rae sat next to him, her body language rigid.

"Anyone else have to talk to the cops?" Bode asked, to no one in particular. "What a waste of time."

Two other couples sat in front of the fire on the opposite side of the fire pit. The four people glanced at him, but no one responded.

Rae, however, made a shushing sound, which seemed to annoy him even more.

"I'm just making conversation," he growled, his voice a lot louder than he probably realized. Or maybe he didn't care.

Reese looked down at her cell phone, hoping to see a message from Cash or...something. As she listened to the couple bicker, she texted Elijah. *Can you keep a secret?*

*For you, always.*

Okay, she seriously adored him. Maybe she would shave Rowan's eyebrows off as revenge for Elijah? *I have a favor. Not job related.*

*Hit me.*

*Cash's ex Isabella Vance is here. I think she's cheating on her current fiancé, John Danforth. Feel like digging for some evidence?*

There was a long pause, then. *Sure. I love this shit. Are we telling Cash?*

*Um…no. The woman's a bitch and I'm feeling petty.* Okay, not entirely true. I mean, she was feeling petty, but she didn't like the woman and if she'd cheated once, she'd cheat again. Some people were just like that, always looking for greener grass.

*No problem. I'll start an encrypted shared file, just for the two of us, so we can both add to it. I'll send you the details later.*

She responded with a bunch of heart-faced emojis, then, *You're the best.*

*True. I also want to stay on your good side.*

*Want me to shave Rowan's eyebrows for you?*

Elijah responded with a purple devil emoji who was smiling evilly.

*I'll take that as a yes. It'll have to be after the job.*

More emojis followed, making Reese smile despite the pit in her stomach. Cash hadn't been gone long, but it felt as if an eternity had passed. Even with the fire going strong, and the heaters, her breath curled in front of her in white little tufts.

"Jesus, you're always nagging." Bode's voice had raised about five octaves in the span of a moment and Reese realized that things were about to get loud and maybe worse.

The blonde stood, her expression hard—oh, she was clearly done with her husband—but Bode grabbed her forearm, yanked the woman back down as she cried out.

As Rae cried out, Reese stood automatically, her drink falling to the ground, but she didn't care. Before she'd even figured out what she was going to do, Cash was suddenly there, striding past Reese and moving toward the other couple like a giant avenging angel.

*Oooooh. Oh, damn.*

"Is there a problem here?" Cash was turned toward Rae, not her husband, his voice soft.

"Yeah, there's a problem. I'm married to a nagging bitch." Bode shoved up from his seat, then body-checked Cash before stalking off.

Reese stood where she was, not moving out of his way even though he was almost twice her size. She bared her teeth at the guy and he stumbled back before cursing under his breath and sidestepping her.

"Do you want us to go with you to talk to Mila about getting another room or anything?" Reese asked as she slid up next to Cash.

Rae looked between the two of them and shook her head—and Reese could see it was taking everything in the woman not to burst into tears.

"Come on, we'll walk you back to your place," Cash murmured, no room for argument in his voice.

Rae didn't respond one way or another, simply dashed away the wetness on her cheeks as she turned away from them, heading in the opposite direction her husband had gone at least.

"He wasn't always like this," she said into the quiet less than a minute later as they headed down the snow-dusted walkway. She'd slowed to walk on Reese's side, had her hands shoved into the pockets of her puffy yellow jacket. "We had a lot of good years, but drinking has taken over his life. I could forgive the cheating—something I never thought I'd say. Because he did it while wasted and barely remembers anything. But he has a mistress and her name is alcohol. It's...tough. I keep thinking that if I love him hard enough, he'll change. And then I wonder what's wrong with me that I can't be enough for him. That something must be wrong with me for him to choose alcohol over me." She let out a shaky, watery laugh as she shook her head. "Sorry. I didn't mean to unload on two very nice strangers. This week has turned into a total shitshow and I just want to go home."

"You don't have to apologize for being human," Reese murmured. "And I'm sorry you're struggling."

"And his drinking has nothing to do with you, for the record." Cash's deep voice was low as he spoke. "My mom was an alcoholic and I used to think the same thing, but addictions are terrible beasts. And once they get their claws in someone, often it's hard to get free. I know you're not asking for advice, but if you haven't looked into Al-Anon, it might help. Even if you're in therapy or even if you divorce him, I still recommend it."

His words surprised Reese because they came from a place of experience.

Rae nodded slowly as they reached her cabin. The lights were on inside, though all the blinds were drawn. "My sister says the same thing."

"She sounds like a smart woman."

The blonde took a long breath, nodded at both of them. "Thank you."

Once she was inside the cabin, Reese slid her hand through Cash's arm. "Should we talk to Mila about this?"

"Yeah. I'd already planned to. Maybe they'll put Rae up in another cabin if she feels unsafe."

"That was kind what you said, your advice."

He lifted a shoulder as they walked back to their cabin. Or she assumed that was where they were going. "I've been there. Not in the same way she is, but living with an addict is hard. Makes you feel like you're going crazy some days."

"I didn't realize, about your mom."

"I don't really talk about her, not to anyone. She died when I was eight. I went to live with my grandma, but she died not too long after so I ended up in foster care." He lifted his shoulder as if it was no big deal, but Reese wanted to pull him into a giant hug.

Since she didn't think that would be welcome, she simply squeezed his forearm and kept walking next to him. "Thank you for telling me."

He shoved out a long breath. "I got the tracker planted. We're good to go."

Apparently they were changing topics. Reese wanted to get more personal with him, but it was clear he was done. And they had a job to do anyway, so she simply said, "Good. Let's stop by Rick and Ava's cabin and go over everything now." Even though no one was out walking around in this cold to overhear them, she still used their cover names.

"Sounds good to me."

## Chapter 20

"So what happens if we get caught?" Cash murmured as they led the quietly whinnying horses out of the stables.

Thankfully Joelle had told them when they could borrow the horses. Though returning them was going to be a lot trickier and was something Reese wasn't going to worry about at the moment. Hopefully Joelle would help them out with that too—she was beyond upset that her friend was dead and wanted to help any way she could, so Reese figured the woman would do just about anything they asked.

One of the stable hands had poker tonight and was planning to be gone for a few hours. Maybe Joelle could stall them if it became necessary? But again, something Reese wasn't going to worry about at the moment. That was a problem for future Reese and right now she was winging it. Because Ben Kingston was up to something and they were going to find out what the hell it was.

"You can just play the rich guy who does what he wants. Make something up about how we wanted to go horseback riding under the moonlight. Rich people do dumb stuff and I guarantee the Kingstons are used to weird behavior."

Cash gave her a sideways glance as they got onto the horses—and damn he looked so much more graceful than she did as he slid on.

"What's that look?" she murmured as she adjusted herself, looking around automatically to see if anyone had spotted them.

Luckily the stables were separate from the cabins and the other entertaining or relaxing areas. Probably to keep the horses separate from the guests for this very reason.

"Nothing. Come on." He took control of his reins and guided his larger horse out.

She kept pace, trotting behind them until they breached the trees onto one of the nearby horse trails. She pulled her phone out to double-check, and yep, Ben Kingston was still headed west. He was going about eight miles an hour so he was clearly being careful on the back trails. Probably because it was night. At least it might allow them to catch up with him to see what he was up to. Cash could watch the tracker on his phone too so if they got separated for some reason, they had a destination.

She followed on her smaller Andalusian, keeping pace as they raced along the cleared path in the direction Ben Kingston had gone. They couldn't follow him directly, would have to use a few out-of-the-way trails so they would avoid seeing any guests.

Or employees.

Which was why they'd dressed appropriately for the cold and to hide their identities. They were both wearing dark toques, face coverings and dark clothing. "Seriously, what was that look back there?" she asked as she rode up next to Cash. Because she wasn't going to let it go.

The path widened, giving them a lot of space. The sound of the horses' hoofbeats and the absolute quiet around them was the only thing she heard. And the quiet absolutely had a sound. There was something about being out in the wild like this, surrounded by remote nature for miles and miles in either direction.

He shot her a sideways glance again, his eyes the only thing visible now that he'd pulled his face mask up to cover his nose. "I'm just trying to figure you out. You grew up with parents who gave you everything and you seem to loathe wealthy people. Even though I'm pretty sure you have a trust. Just unsure where I stand with you, honestly. Not sure if you're judging me or what."

*Oh god.* "No! I'm not judging you." And how was he not breathing hard? Or she didn't think he was. But as she urged her horse to keep pace with his, and to freaking talk through the mask, she sucked in a hard breath. "I know I can be kind of judgy sometimes and that's a me problem, not you. I...*have* dealt with my share of rich assholes. Some from boarding school and some from my parents' orbit. I understand that everyone, regardless of socioeconomic background, has life shit to deal with. I one hundred percent get that..."

He nodded that she should follow him to the left at the upcoming fork, but still let her talk.

"But in my life experiences, I've seen a whole lot of entitlement from people in my parents' orbit. And it's more of them than not. Like eighty percent more. It's exhausting and gross, so yeah, sometimes I lump people together. I know it's not right. I mean, look at Jesse, jeez. The man is a saint. And you aren't even really a billionaire anymore because you just keep giving money away. Now you're here with me in the freezing cold woods because you're trying to make a difference for a woman who only a small handful of people will miss. So I'm sorry if I've ever directed my judgment at you. I promise I don't mean it and I'll try to do better."

He tugged his mask down as they reached another bend. This time three separate trails split before them. Cash motioned toward the middle one, his breath curling out in little white wisps. "With the exception of our first meeting, I've never felt judged by you. And even that didn't feel personal. Also, how do you know that I keep giving away my money?"

Ooooh, she was so glad it was dark out and she had a mask on so he wouldn't be able to see the warmth flooding her cheeks. "Ah, lucky guess?" She dug her heels into her horse, urging her to go faster.

"No way. Are you stalking me?" Cash grinned as he rode up next to her, not bothering to pull his face mask back up. He looked quite pleased with himself in that moment.

*Ugh.* "I'm not stalking you, per se. Just...fine, whatever, maybe I'm a little curious about you!" And yeah, maybe she'd stalked him online a little. It wasn't like she'd been sitting outside his house with night vision binoculars.

"For the record, I'll tell you anything you want to know," he rumbled, his voice dropping a few octaves. "So what did you find out about me?" He pulled the thick, insulated covering back up, likely because of how cutting the wind was, but she could *hear* the grin in his voice.

She rolled her eyes but found herself smiling regardless. "Just that you give to really worthy causes." He'd built libraries, had donated ambulances to something like five hundred rural areas across the country that wouldn't have easy access to a hospital otherwise. He also had a bunch of scholarships for kids who were first-generation college attendees or foster kids. And those two criteria often went together. But he was just giving away money and opportunities like candy and it hit her right in her feels. Because it was easy for people to say that they'd be generous if they had the money—he was actually doing it.

She'd wanted to lump him into a certain category because of her own bias, much to her shame. And he didn't deserve that.

"And you don't even let people know about," she added. "Which tells me you've got a terrible PR team, or you want to donate without any fanfare. I'm guessing it's the latter. For the record, you're pretty damn wonderful, Cash Pierce."

He looked over at her as they slowed at the next fork, but didn't respond. And she wasn't sure what to make of his intense look, of the way his eyes swept over her for a moment.

Because just as quickly, he pulled away from her, leaving her to follow as the trail thinned. The icy air chilled the sliver of exposed skin on her face, but a surge of adrenaline punched through her as she digested his expression.

That look he'd given her.

Because she wasn't misinterpreting anything. Not when it came to him.

As the wind picked up, she hunched over, glad for him to take the lead, especially since little drifts of snow had started to fall. *Great, just great.* She wasn't wired for this kind of weather. Nope, she preferred easy winters where it snowed maybe once or twice—or maybe not at all.

She wasn't sure how long they'd been riding, maybe another twenty minutes, when he slowed and lifted a fist. A signal that they were getting close or something was going on.

She pulled her phone out, looked at the blinking dot. Oh, they were *really* close. Kingston was somewhere to the west of them through a bunch of forest.

The falling snow had thankfully petered off, but she didn't think the reprieve would last long.

Cash tugged his mask down as he turned to her, then motioned it was time to dismount.

Nodding, she followed suit, glad to be on her own two feet again. She stretched slightly as she pulled out her NVBs and long-range camera. Cash did the same, pulling out his own NVBs before he tied his horse directly off the trail.

"Will they be okay?" she whispered, hating to leave them. Hell, she hated that they'd brought the animals out in the cold, even if they seemed unfazed by it. They had on thick coverings and leg warmers, which shouldn't have been as adorable as it was.

"Yeah. I left the reins loose. If something happens, they know the way home."

"Okay. I'm texting Rowan," she murmured as she shot off a quick message. *We're about to get in place. Will keep you updated.* She tucked her phone away after double-checking that the volume was off. "I'm ready."

He nodded, his binoculars secured to his belt. "Since I have tactical experience, I'm taking lead." The way he said it sounded as if he expected her to argue.

But this wasn't her expertise. She was good at computers, good at piecing stuff together, but this was not her world. Normally she was a voice on the other end of a comm, feeding intel. "Of course. You lead, I follow."

He paused, as if he wanted to say more, then simply nodded and took off on foot through the woods.

Unlike the trail, which had been cleared, the forest had a couple feet of snow. Her feet sank into the softness and she was glad for the hardcore winter gear Cash had insisted they bring.

The way the man moved through the woods shouldn't be so sexy, but he moved like a skilled operator. And she'd seen his other moves, knew very well how talented he was.

Ten minutes later Cash held up his hand again, then motioned that they were slowing down. The trees were still crowded and thick, but she could hear the rumble of an engine nearby. Sounded as if it was simply idling.

Her heart rate kicked up automatically as they moved closer to the sound. And that was when she heard another engine getting closer.

Cash picked up his pace so she did the same, following in the depressions of his boots in the snow to move faster. A few minutes later, as the trees started to thin slightly, he slowed again so she did the same.

Then he stretched out on his stomach and signaled for her to do the same.

As she lay next to him, he pulled out his NVBs and held them up so she pulled out her long-range IR camera. Looking through it, she slowly passed over the trees in her way before... *There.*

Ben Kingston was visible through the forest leaning against the front of his ATV. He'd turned off the headlights as another man stopped his own ATV in front of his, killed the lights. Nope, it was two men she realized. Someone was in the passenger seat.

She snapped a few pictures even though she wasn't sure if she'd manage to pull any IDs for the men. But the company camera was incredible—stalker, TMZ level that could take pictures from a mile or more away. It was waterproof and mostly drop-proof, thankfully. And right now she was getting clear images of Ben Kingston talking to one unknown man.

The other was staying in the ATV behind the wheel, bundled up in his coat and gloves, his face not visible.

They were too far away to hear, but Cash eased out the small parabolic mic he'd packed and slid on his earphones. She wanted to ask what he was hearing but knew better. So she kept taking pictures until Cash shifted slightly, his body language changing. She couldn't actually see all his muscles tighten, but everything about him was stiffer, as if he was ready to jump up at a moment's notice.

Ben and the man he was talking to had raised their voices. She was still too far away, but clearly something had changed, a shout carrying on the air. Then the man held up his hands as if trying to placate Ben.

Ben nodded, then headed back to his ATV, grabbed a duffel bag.

The other man walked to the back of his ATV as well and, oh, the driver was now getting out. The man was a bit taller than the other two, and even though she couldn't see his face because of his mask, she snapped a picture of him. She might be able to figure out his height by comparing it to the model of ATV. It wasn't much, but if she ID'd the other guy, he'd have known associates in the system.

"We need to get out of here," Cash whispered.

She glanced at him and saw he'd pulled his mask down slightly. "They've been arguing about money and distribution areas. This is definitely a drug deal."

Yeah, she'd figured as much, given the big-ass duffel bag.

She'd started to put her camera down when Ben rounded his ATV, then shot the man he'd been arguing with point-blank in the chest.

*Pop. Pop.* The sound echoed slightly but was muted because of the suppressor.

And holy shit, things had just changed big-time. She forgot to breathe as she digested what had just happened in front of her.

The other man who'd been in the passenger seat made a move to reach for a weapon, but Ben shouted something at him. Reese kept snapping pictures as Kingston held the gun on the guy, motioning with it.

The man picked up what was likely a bag of drugs, then put it in the back of Ben's ATV. Then to her surprise, Ben tossed the bag he had at the guy.

"Let's go." Cash gently tugged on her forearm and she realized he'd already put his small mic and headphones away. He plucked the camera out of her hand before she could respond, then moved to his feet, tugging her up with him.

Heart racing now, she hurried with him, wanting to put as much distance between Ben Kingston and them as possible. As she raced alongside Cash, she pulled out her phone and dropped a pin to the others so they'd have a near exact location of the murder.

"Hey!" A shout sounded far behind them and she turned, saw the lights to the ATV flaring to life.

"Someone might have seen us," Cash hissed, grabbing her arm and pulling her along even faster.

*Shit, shit, shit.* She didn't bother trying to be stealthy now, her boots kicking up snow as she ran. She heard the engine rev as she and Cash burst through the trees onto the trail where they'd left the horses.

Cash grabbed the reins to her horse, then slapped his butt, sending him in the direction of Kingston. The horse whinnied loudly and sprinted away from them.

"Come on, in front of me," he ordered, basically tossing her on before she could think about protesting. She wasn't even sure if the horse could hold them, but it was a beast and Cash seemed sure so she was trusting him.

He slid behind her, let out a harsh order, dug his heels in and the horse took off.

She hunkered down, sweat beading along her spine and down her neck despite the cold.

An engine revved behind them somewhere and she couldn't turn to see. *Oh god.* Kingston *had* seen them. Maybe they'd been caught in the headlights?

"I've got us. Hold on," Cash growled in her ear as they suddenly veered off the trail into the thick of the forest. Because of the crescent moon and stars blanketing the sky through the trees, she could see enough and it was clear the horse did as well when it jumped over a fallen tree.

She held back a yelp as it landed on all fours. At least the ATV couldn't follow them. Or she didn't think it could.

"Is he following us?"

Three shots rent the air, one after the other, and a tree splintered five feet from them, wood flying everywhere.

On instinct, she started to duck, but Cash was blocking her.

"We're fine. We're going to lose him in just a minute." Cash was leaning forward now, covering her body with his as they jumped over another fallen tree.

That was when she realized the sound of the engine had faded. The staccato beat of her heart didn't ease much, but she ducked down lower and managed to turn around to see behind them. She couldn't make out much through the woods.

"Call the others. Tell them what's going on." Cash's voice was close to her ear as they cleared the forest into one of the other trails. One they'd rode in on earlier.

Only this time they'd cut their time in half because she recognized where they were. Maybe only a mile from the stables.

Holding her phone close, she called Rowan since he was the last contact in her phone, and told him everything.

"Hey, where are you going?" she asked as alarm punched through her. Cash had missed the turnoff to the stables.

"Can't go back to the stables. If he's working with anyone, he'll have called ahead. We're going to loop around to one of the other trails, then hoof it on foot back to the cabin. We just need to avoid any cameras."

"That's easy enough," she murmured, pulling out her phone. She'd left a back door open into the camera system. She hadn't wanted to use this method because it would be clear someone had hacked into the system and eventually they'd patch it. But desperate times and all that.

She grunted as Cash veered them off the trail and into another thicket of forest, the jostling making it difficult to work. But she got it done.

"Okay, we're good to go. Cameras are off. I've let the others know as well."

"Good. Are you ready?" Cash asked as they neared the original trail they'd followed Kingston on, that very first day. Yesterday, she realized. Jesus, they'd only been here two days, but it felt a hell of a lot longer.

"Yep," she murmured as Cash slowed then stopped the horse.

He helped her off, then patted the giant horse's mane. "Good girl. You're a rock star and we're thankful you saved us," he murmured into her mane. "Now go home." He patted her butt and she trotted off as if she'd understood him completely, heading toward the stables.

In that moment, Reese realized that she'd fallen hard for Cash whether she wanted to admit it or not.

And she also realized something else. "You're shot!"

## Chapter 21

"Just got a text, the security cameras are down," Adalyn whispered from her hiding spot with Rowan behind one of the storage sheds about fifty yards from the stables.

"Good. Oh, there's one of the horses." He was peering around the corner of the shed.

"Just one?" She knew they'd taken two out and she hated the thought of the animals being lost, or worse.

"Yeah. The other will turn up. Oh...you hear that?"

She stood still, the night air eerily quiet since they were a decent distance from the main cabins and most people were in for the night. A moment later she heard the soft whine of an engine. "Can you see anything?"

"Nope...wait. Lights in the distance, coming from one of the trails."

She moved up beside him, but ducked below him as she peered around the corner. Her breath curled in front of her as she spotted the twin lights flashing through the woods. "How are we going to handle this? We've got the location of the body. Are we calling the local police?"

"I doubt it. At least not yet," Rowan murmured as he eased back with her.

The ATV was headed toward the stables, and while they were hidden, they didn't want to risk getting seen on accident.

"There was another guy there. Reese said he might have taken the body with him," Rowan added.

"There will still be forensic evidence," Adalyn murmured. She was used to doing jobs a certain way, and while she understood why they were undercover looking for the missing woman, someone had been killed. And Reese and Cash were eyewitnesses.

"I know. But we're essentially in foreign territory." Rowan's voice was pitched low as he peered around the corner again. "And according to Mia Williams, Ben Kingston is friends with powerful people and law enforcement."

The engine sounded like it was idling now. "Yeah, true. Shit. I don't like any of this."

"Yeah, me neither. Check this out."

She slid up next to him, peered around the shed again and saw Ben Kingston grabbing a big duffel from the back of his ATV. He disappeared into the stables for about a minute, then strode back out holding his cell phone to his ear as he jumped back into the ATV. His body language was angry, controlled as he zoomed off, kicking up snow as he tore across the pathway toward the cabins and main gathering area.

"I'm going to grab that duffel," Rowan whispered before he ducked around the corner, using the shadows and darkness to sprint across the open spread of land.

She ran after him on instinct, wanting to cover him in case another threat popped up. She wasn't armed other than some bear spray she'd grabbed when they'd first arrived. She'd taken it under the guise of carrying it with her on hikes, but it was her weapon while she was here.

"What are you doing?" Rowan demanded as she slid up next to him, plastering her back against the barn as she reached him.

"Watching your six, dumbass."

He just muttered something before he eased toward the partially open stable door. A few horses whinnied, but the lights were dim and it was clear things were quiet for the night. Though Kingston hadn't even put the horse, Cookie, back in her stable before he'd run off.

"There aren't many places to stash his bag," she whispered as they moved inside together.

She stepped on bits of fallen hay as she eyed the door of what had to be the storage area. She pulled on the heavy-duty lock, cursed to herself. "We'll need bolt cutters to get this off."

"Move." Rowan nudged her to the side and before she realized what he was doing, he hauled back and slammed his boot right under the door handle. It splintered open under his force, wood tearing off as it flew open. The base of the lock ripped right off where it had been secured on the frame, the screws popping off. The lock itself was still locked, but it hadn't been secure enough to remain in place.

She looked into the storage room. A duffel bag had been tossed onto one of the lower shelves.

"Bingo." Rowan snatched it up, then held up a finger to his mouth.

That was when she heard the voice. Not agitated, but soothing. What the hell?

She quietly eased out of the supply closet and spotted Mila, with her back to them, gently calming down Cookie.

*Come on*, she mouthed, walking backward toward the doors they'd snuck in through.

Rowan moved quickly, his movements ghost silent for someone so large.

Mila was still making soothing sounds to the horse as she led it to the stable. As she did, the woman's cell phone rang, further distracting her so Adalyn moved fast, ducking out of the stable, Rowan hot on her heels.

"What the hell is going on?" Mila demanded, and for a moment Adalyn froze, her heart in her throat.

Had they been caught?

But the woman continued and it was clear she was on a phone call. "Two of our horses are out and the damn cameras have gone down. This is bullshit…"

"Run for the trees," he whispered. "We only have a small window."

Adalyn fell in line next to him, her hiking boots kicking up snow as they sprinted to the trees, which were about a football field's length past the storage shed they'd used for cover.

Once they breached the cover of forest, Rowan slowed, barely out of breath as he set the bag on the cold ground, unzipped it.

Her stomach tightened as she stared down at the contents. Hundreds of plastic baggies filled the duffel.

"You know what this is?" Rowan asked, looking back up at her as he zipped it up.

"Likely counterfeit oxy. It'll be laced with fentanyl and heroin. I recognize the stamps on the bags—Chavez cartel. Ben Kingston might not be working directly with the cartel, but he's working with one of their distributors at least. But with this amount…he's moving some serious product."

"And he just killed someone."

"But left the other alive," Adalyn added. "We need to talk to Cash and Reese face-to-face, but we can't bring this back to the cabin."

Rowan frowned as he looked down at the offending bag. "No we can't. There's no way to hide this shit. I say we bury it out here." He looked up at the sky as snow started falling in earnest. "The snow will cover our tracks and any disturbance."

She nodded as she looked past him into the forest. "The ground's going to be too hard to break and we don't have tools, but the snow's already thick enough. We can bury it in the snow, pin the location and retrieve it later once we figure out what the hell we're going to do with it."

Rowan gave a resigned nod. "Works for me."

It took them twenty minutes to hike deeper into the woods and find a good spot, then another hour to hoof it back to their cabin.

By the time they managed to sneak back, Adalyn was soaked through to her long johns and miserable. But at least the snow had provided a hell of a cover for them while they hid the drugs, then trekked back the long way.

When she stepped into the kitchen, she froze to find Cash and Reese there, Cash with his shirt off, a bandage around his upper right arm.

"Someone was out doing patrols so we came here. And Cash was shot," Reese growled.

## CHAPTER 22

"I wasn't shot," Cash said dryly. Even if he could admit that he'd liked Reese's fussing over him. "It barely skimmed me, just tore up my jacket. And I'm going to have to destroy it anyway in case Kingston recognizes it."

"Same," Reese added. "We bagged up all our clothes and hid them away in the attic. Sorry for borrowing yours." She motioned to her jeans and sweater as she scooted closer to Cash on the couch.

Ever since she realized he'd been "injured," she'd kept only a foot or two away from him, as if worried he was going to fall over. He wasn't sure if he should be insulted, but he loved that she cared so much.

"It's fine." Adalyn sat on the couch across from them, her expression tense.

They'd started the fire so the living room was toasty. The setup was the same as their living room with only a few changes in the space, namely the art. But it was clear they'd used the same artist.

Rowan sat right in front of Cash on the sturdy coffee table. "We've got some shit to tell you but let me see the wound first."

Oh right, the man had been a medic. "I'm fine," Cash muttered but tugged his borrowed sweater off anyway and twisted slightly. Reese had cleaned his wound—which was basically a scratch—and then bandaged it, all while cursing Ben Kingston under her breath.

Rowan gently peeled back the bandage and then nodded in satisfaction. "Ah, just a scratch. You don't even need stitches or steri-strips for this."

Reese made a scoffing sound, but he ignored her—even if he loved how much she cared.

"That's what I've been saying. Now what happened with you guys?" Because they'd been gone a while.

Rowan looked back at Adalyn, nodded once. Whatever tension had been between them before wasn't completely gone, but they'd been working together like pros the last two days.

"We found a shitload of drugs," Adalyn said before launching into what they'd found and where they'd hidden it.

When she was done, he and Reese both cursed.

"Clearly there's a hell of a lot more going on here than a missing...murdered woman," Cash said into the quiet.

"The murder of Aubry might not even be related to all this," Reese added. "And we need to bring in some big guns at this point. Anonymously is fine, but the DEA needs to be contacted."

"We could reach out to Hazel. She'll likely have contacts," Rowan offered.

Reese shook her head. "Pretty sure Skye has direct contacts with the DEA." She glanced at her phone. "I hate calling her this late."

Rowan snorted. "She'll be pissed if you don't."

Cash snorted his own agreement as he stood, stretched and put his sweater back on. While dressing he saw a flash of blue lights through a small gap in the blinds. The others continued talking as he moved to one of the blinds and eased it back. At least three uniformed individuals were walking around and one was coming this way.

Cash stepped away from the window. "Guys, a couple sheriff's trucks are here. Everyone strip and get into robes, now. We only have a minute or so at most. Reese grab me one from upstairs," he said as he started stripping off his sweater once again, and this time his jeans.

It was clear the others either wanted to argue or ask him what the hell was going on, but he hurried for the kitchen, grabbed four glasses of wine and opened the nearest bottle.

As the others moved upstairs, he set up a small tray and added some cheese and fruit, setting it on the coffee table along with the wine. Then he opened up another bottle, emptied that one down the sink so it would appear as if they'd gone through at least one bottle and were working on the second.

Reese beat the others downstairs and handed him a fluffy white robe that was a mirror to one in their cabin. She had on a matching one, though hers fell to her feet. She eyed the cheese and wine on the coffee table, raised her eyebrows. "Ahh," she murmured in understanding, then went to the sound system and turned on low, soothing classical music.

Rowan and Adalyn returned a moment later, right as a pounding on the front door sounded.

"So...are we really leaning into the whole orgy thing?" Rowan asked, taking in the scene Cash had set and understanding immediately what he intended.

"Or wife swap. Whatever. Either way is a good alibi," Cash said, pulling Reese onto his lap as he sat. "Grab the door."

Rowan sighed, but nodded and stepped out into the hallway heading toward the front door. There was a rumble of voices, then moments later Detective Valerie Lippman and the detective she'd been with before, Frank Conroy, appeared in the entryway.

Conroy took the lead, looking at the three of them, his gaze landing on the food and drinks as he stepped deeper into the living room. "Good evening, folks. Apologies for the late drop-in."

"Good evening," Cash said while the women murmured the same. "What brings you out here tonight? Is everything okay?"

"A couple of the Kingstons' horses have been stolen so we're talking to everyone."

"Oh no," Reese murmured. "Are the horses okay?"

Conroy focused on her and it took all Cash's self-control not to shove her behind him, to hide her away. The instinct to protect her from everything was damn near overwhelming. And as far as he was concerned, the cops might be involved in whatever this shit was. Now that he thought about it, if Kingston was running drugs through his place, or acting as a middleman, having the local cops in his pocket would make life a lot easier for him. Not to mention what Mia Williams had told Reese.

"Horses are fine," the detective murmured. "Now who are you all exactly? I know we talked to some of you before but please refresh my memory?"

Oh, he was lying, he knew exactly who they were. Cash could read it on the man's face.

So he took over even as he played along. "I'm Cash Pierce and this is my fiancé, Reese Sinclair. Her parents have done some lobbying for your governor, I believe." He looked at Reese as if to confirm, even though he was lying his ass off.

Reese simply smiled at him.

Cash looked back at the detective. "So if you want to know if we took your horses, the answer is no. Besides, this place has a bunch of security cameras. Why aren't you just looking at the Kingstons' security?"

Valerie stepped up then, her expression a lot softer than Conroy's. "There's been a glitch with the system. I think it's the cold weather. It affects things here sometimes, especially our satellite connections. We're not trying to bother anyone, we're just checking around to see if anyone saw anything really. So have you been here for a while?"

Cash nodded. "Yep, the last few hours. I met up with Mr. Kingston about something about oh, nine, I guess. Then Reese and I headed back here."

"And you've been here the entire time?" Conroy asked this time, his tone hard. "Doing what exactly?"

Reese cleared her throat delicately, as if embarrassed. And Adalyn did the same as she reached for her glass of wine.

"Having sex mostly," Rowan said before Cash could answer. "We met them on the plane and hit it off. Turns out they like to swap partners so we've been…getting to know each other."

Conroy's expression was priceless and he seemed to realize for the first time that they were all in robes. Valerie, however, smothered a smile. So apparently she was a bit more observant than her partner.

Conroy stepped back, clearly disgusted with them, his shoulders tight. "We're sorry to have bothered you."

Valerie nodded politely at them. "If you remember seeing anything, just let us know," she murmured. "And if you don't want your neighbors to know what you're up to, maybe don't head back to your cabin just yet. We're going to be here for a while."

"We have no shame about our lifestyle." Cash grinned as he stretched his arm across the back of the couch.

She nodded again, and he could see she was either fighting a smile or an eye roll before she followed after her partner.

Rowan walked them out, locked up, then returned and snorted out a laugh. "I'd been kidding about the orgy thing, but I'm pretty sure it worked."

Cash shrugged. "Make someone uncomfortable enough and they'll want to get away from you as quickly as possible."

"He was so disgusted by us," Adalyn said on a laugh before she took a sip of wine.

"It's weird that they're out here so quickly," Reese added. "And I can't imagine that the Kingstons called them at close to one in the morning over some horses. They'd handle it later, especially since it sounds like the horses are back already. This is about the missing drugs. I'd bet my last dollar. They want to know who took their stuff."

Cash nodded. "Yeah, I think they're going to end up searching our cabins tomorrow. We'll need to dispose of our clothes before then."

"We'll need to stash our NVBs and other gear somewhere."

"There are a few empty cabins. We could break into one and tuck our stuff away in an attic. Not the best plan but it keeps our gear out of the elements. And I don't think we're going to be here much longer," Rowan said. "We're going to have to bring someone else in. Because that amount of drugs is serious. They're either working directly with the cartel or a middle man who distributes for them."

"There was a bust over in Butte not too long ago tied to one of the cartels." Cash remembered reading something about it. "Maybe we could see who the lead agent was, anonymously contact them."

"Ooh, I like that." Reese nodded in agreement. "Anything that keeps our company off the radar of anyone involved with this, the better. We might be able to retain our covers that way."

Rowan and Adalyn both nodded, and when Reese stood, Cash followed. At the end of the day, he was going to follow that woman anywhere.

## CHAPTER 23

Reese leaned against the door to their cabin after locking the deadbolt, glad to be alone with him even if she was still reeling from being chased and shot at. "I feel like things spiraled so quickly."

Cash, however, just shrugged, all nonchalant as he started the fireplace. And she found herself annoyed that he was so blasé about his own life.

"You could have been killed," she snapped, exhaustion punching through her hard. And something else she still hadn't come back down from.

Fear. Fear that she'd almost lost Cash.

"Please, I'm fine." He headed for the kitchen, stripping off his borrowed sweater once again. He stretched once before he looked in the fridge. "I am pretty hungry. Probably couldn't call for service though, this late," he muttered, seemingly to himself more than her.

"Are you serious right now?" She stomped her boots off by the door, realizing how childish she likely looked. But she didn't care. "How can you be so casual about all this?" She yanked her coat off as she joined him in the kitchen, threw it on the countertop. "What if he'd been a better shot? He could have hit you in the back, puncturing your lung! Or, or…oh god, your spine. This could have been so much worse." Damn it, she knew she was starting to spiral but couldn't stop it, not with fear bubbling up inside her so fresh and hot it burned her throat.

He shut the fridge as he turned to face her. "I'm fine and none of that happened. And I've been shot at *and* stabbed before. Everything is okay." His voice was annoyingly calm as he stood there shirtless, his bandage on display as a reminder of his injury.

His brush with death.

"Well I'm not okay. And I know it's not about me, but I need a hug." She'd been running on adrenaline the last couple hours, or at least it felt like it. "I barely made it through that conversation with the cops. And I've never struggled like that before on a job." And she knew exactly why she was having such a hard time keeping her shit together.

Because he'd been hurt.

"Come here." Cash pulled her into his arms as he made soothing sounds.

"You shouldn't be making me feel better," she muttered into his chest, hugging him tight. He smelled so good, and his body against hers woke up everything inside her—and then she felt like a giant pervert for noticing at all.

"So I should be making you feel worse?"

"That's not what I meant." She squeezed him once to make her point.

He buried his face against the top of her head. "Reese, it's okay. Everything's going to be fine. We're going to call Skye in a minute and—"

"I don't care about any of that. I was worried about *you*, Cash. You. I thought... If anything happened to you..." She swallowed hard, unable to go on. She was just glad she had her face hidden so he couldn't see her expression or the tears she was desperately fighting. She wasn't a crier, and definitely not on a job. But here she was, about to let the dam break free. *No.* She refused to let that happen.

But he pulled back slightly and tucked his hand under her chin, making her look at him.

"No, don't look at me. Stupid tears," she growled, trying to pull away from him, to avoid his gaze.

But he wasn't having it. "Don't cry." There was a note of panic in his voice as he cupped her cheeks and swiped away her tears.

"I'm not crying. You're crying."

He laughed lightly as he bent down, kissed one cheek, then the other, and oooohhh, she just let go of whatever control she had. That thin thread snapped free as she leaned into him, searching out his mouth right as he crushed his to hers. There was no more fighting this.

She arched into him as he claimed her mouth with a scorching need she felt to her core.

But suddenly he pulled back, his eyes blazing. "For the record, I would never share you, never swap with anyone. I know we were acting but I want that crystal clear. I will never, *ever* share you."

Her knees actually weakened at his words but he took over, hoisting her up onto the counter with ease.

"Your arm—"

"Forget my arm," he growled as he reached for the hem of her sweater and started lifting it up.

She didn't think to protest, because she wanted whatever happened between them now, would hold on tight to the memory. Cool air rushed over her as he tossed her clothing away, but he wasn't done.

With his eyes on hers, he unbuttoned her borrowed jeans and tugged them and her panties off in one swoop.

"I'm going to taste you and then I'm going to fuck you."

She sucked in a breath at his blunt words right as he kissed her again, his tongue teasing and sensual as he finally slipped off her bra, the final bit of her clothing. Instead of feeling insecure in front of him, as she had in the past, she savored the way he stared at her, seemed to drink her all in. Because the way he looked at her... she could see that he wanted her as much as she wanted him.

Desperate to touch all of him, she spread her fingers over his bare stomach, enjoying the feel of his hard body beneath her fingertips. After their night together, she'd been obsessing about touching him again, feeling all his raw power underneath her.

She'd felt it earlier on the horse when he'd so easily tossed her up onto it, then just taken over. And seeing him in action, so in control over everything, was a bigger turn-on than she'd ever imagined. None of her exes were like him.

Hell, she wasn't sure she'd *ever* known anyone like him, period. He was so capable and take-charge, and ooooh, her inner walls clenched automatically as he slid his big palm up her thigh, pressing it outward.

As she spread her legs for him, she reached for the button of his jeans, but he was having none of that.

"Not yet," he murmured against her mouth as he slid a finger inside her, teasing, testing.

She rolled her hips against him, sucking in a breath at the feel of him pushing deeper, deeper. "I want to feel all of you." Because she had absolutely no self-control and wanted what she wanted. Right now.

"Not yet." There was a hint of amusement in his voice as he eased her back. "Now lie down."

"What?" She stared at him for a moment.

"Lie. Down. I'm going to taste you."

*Oh. God. Those words.* Her inner walls clenched around his finger as she stared at him. Because she felt the intensity of his look all the way to her core, knew that he was going to enjoy going down on her. "I get to taste you too," she whispered because now had to be about both of them.

"Whatever you want, princess."

She should not like when he called her princess, but oh, it did something to her insides, as if he was claiming her in some way. So she lay back on the countertop even as she scooted down slightly to give him better access.

And the growl he made was practically feral as he buried his face between her legs. The sudden intrusion of having his mouth between her folds, sucking on her clit, was almost too much to bear.

She arched off the island top as he slid another finger inside her and began thrusting in a slow, steady rhythm.

"You've got such a perfect pussy." Another demanding growl against her that reverberated to her core.

She shouldn't love his words either, but oh she did. And absolutely loved it coming from him. She couldn't talk right now, much less think straight as he thrust his fingers inside her again, over and over.

"You're going to come all over my face," he rasped out, his words an order.

She jerked again, her inner walls clenching as he sucked on her clit now, even harder.

"Cash." She knew from experience that he loved when she cried out his name. Well he was in luck because it was about the only thing she could manage as pleasure threatened to overload her senses. "I'm so close." And now she sounded like she was begging, but whatever, she *was* begging. She was desperate for release, desperate for the kind of pleasure he could give her, and he'd learned her body so quickly.

She should feel vulnerable splayed out like this for him, but she felt powerful in a way she'd never experienced except with him as he pleasured her. Because he did it in a way that told her he truly loved this, that he didn't want to be anywhere but with her.

And the feeling was mutual, because the thought of being separated from him was too much. She wasn't sure what to think of it, but something in her bones told her that she was going to know this man for the rest of her life. Yep, she'd fallen so damn hard for him and knew there was no coming back. Her faux engagement ring sparkled under the dim lighting of the kitchen and her breath caught in her throat as she imagined it being real.

"Come. Now." A demanding order that reverberated through her.

And when he sucked on her clit again, she surged into orgasm, pleasure punching out to all her nerve endings as he continued his delicious form of torture until she fell limp against the countertop, barely able to catch her breath.

But he was definitely not done, and neither was she. As she started to sit, he scooped her up from the countertop, but when he headed for the stairs, she shook her head.

"By the fire," she murmured as she nibbled against his neck, moved on to his ear.

She hated that he was carrying her at all with his injured arm, but he was determined and stubborn. So she was going to pick her battles, and right now she wanted him naked and inside her more than anything.

He changed course immediately, the heat in his eyes scorching as he cut a path for the living room.

"On the couch," she ordered. "You sit."

He looked as if he wanted to argue, but perched on the edge of the couch as she straddled him.

The fire crackled next to them, casting shadows that played off his ridiculously handsome face as she reached between his legs and rubbed her palm over his covered erection. Oh yeah, his clothes would be coming off *right* now.

He groaned against her touch, rolling his hips up to meet her. "We could have been doing this for weeks. Hell, months," he growled against her mouth.

And he wasn't wrong. The attraction between them had sparked during their first meeting. It had been the beginning of her obsession, one that was still going strong. One she was pretty sure was never going to wane, if the way she felt now was any indication.

She bit his bottom lip in response, making him groan against her. "Jeans. Off."

Without pause he shucked his jeans and boxer briefs with efficiency. Then he tried to take over, because of course he did. It seemed to be the way he was wired, but she was having none of that.

"No. It's my turn to have my way with you." She straddled him, loving the skin-to-skin sensation of being so connected to him. Because with Cash, everything had changed. There was a different level of intimacy with him than she'd ever experienced.

"You can do whatever you want to me." His gaze was on her mouth as he gripped her hips in that dominating way of his that sent a flood of heat between her legs. It didn't seem to matter that he was underneath her and she was determined to be in charge, he was still trying to take control.

She reached between their bodies and grasped his thick length as she leaned down to brush her mouth over his. As she stroked him, he groaned into her mouth with a desperation that mirrored her own.

"I want to be inside you," he growled, nipping her bottom lip.

And she wanted to tease him, but...screw it. She wanted him inside her too. "We're not done after this," she rasped out, wanting to make it clear that this wasn't over, not by a long shot. And she didn't care if she *did* sound desperate. She wanted everything about tonight to be real, honest.

"Oh, we're definitely not done, princess." Still clutching onto her with those powerful, callused hands, he lifted her up even as she pushed up on her knees.

Before she could ease down onto his thick length, he thrust upward as she was moving down on him. Her head rolled back as he completely filled her, the sensation of being stretched by him sending out little pings of pleasure to all her nerve endings.

She hadn't forgotten how big he was, but, okay, maaaaybe she had. She stayed where she was, with him buried to the hilt, enjoying the ragged breaths he was dragging in. He was just as affected as her at least.

Slowly, she started rolling her hips against his, her knees digging into the couch beneath them as she got used to his size.

He held on to her as if he was afraid she'd run, and hell, maybe that was fair considering she had before. But she wasn't running anymore. Not after tonight.

When he dipped his head to her breast, sucked her already hard nipple into his mouth, it was like he set something off in her.

She started riding him in a rhythm that was as old as time, but somehow felt bright and new and all theirs. With each thrust of him inside her, she felt more and more connected to this wonderful man. The connection between them sparked, expanded as they found pleasure in each other once again.

It didn't take long for another climax to build inside her, much to her surprise. She'd always been a "one and done" until he came along. Or a "one and another a couple hours later." But Cash had this magic ability to wring all the pleasure out of her, then go back for more. Then again.

"I'm close," she panted as he switched breasts.

"Good." He sucked her other nipple, a little harder this time, and her inner walls tightened around him at the pleasure.

So he did it again, and again, clearly determined to take everything she had. With each tug, she raced closer and closer to orgasm until he gently bit down on her sensitive bud.

The action set her off, sending another wave of pleasure spiraling through her. She grabbed his face, crushed her mouth to his in a bid to claim him as he met her stroke for manic stroke.

As she rolled her hips against his, he thrust harder and faster into her until her climax fully hit. Little black spots danced behind her eyes as she grabbed onto that pleasure, rode the wave of her orgasm while he came with her.

"Reese." He growled her name as he buried his face against her neck, the heat of his breath, the desperate way he called out her name, extending her orgasm until she could barely breathe.

Eventually she came down from her high to find him watching her with pure satisfaction. "You look very pleased with yourself," she murmured, nipping his earlobe.

He rolled his hips once, his half-hard cock still inside her. "I just watched you come twice so I am *very* pleased."

Her cheeks heated at his words. And in that moment she remembered his injury. "Oh god, your arm—"

"Is fine," he said on a laugh. "I love that you're so worried about me, but I swear I'm good. Hell, better than good. I'm fantastic now that I'm inside you again."

Her inner walls tightened at his words, which just made him grin even wider. And she savored him, memorized the way he looked so at ease, so damn wonderful she wanted to cry for how perfect this moment was.

Soon they needed to make phone calls to their boss and deal with the mess here, but for this one moment in time she was going to treasure every little thing.

## Chapter 24

"This is interesting." Reese nodded to her laptop as she scrolled through the ongoing texts between Valerie Lippman and Mila Kingston.

It had been a couple hours since they returned to their cabin and they'd retired to the bedroom not too long ago. Because every time they looked out the window, the cops were still walking around talking to people. Apparently they didn't care that it was well into the early hours of the morning. The fact that Ben Kingston didn't care about disturbing the guests told Reese all she needed to know. This was not about horses. And there was no way they could attempt to move their discarded clothing or even think about moving the drugs. No, they needed to stay put.

Valerie: *I'm just following orders.*

Burner phone (assumed Mila Kingston): *It's ridiculous that the two of you are out here disturbing our guests this early. I could have easily handled this! The horses are fine.*

Valerie: *I agree, but I'm still just following orders. If you have a problem, take it up with your husband. He's the one who called the sheriff, who in turn called me and told me to get my ass over here asap.*

There was a veeeerrrry long pause.

Burner phone (assumed Mila Kingston): *You're right, I'm sorry. I'm just frustrated and don't understand what's going on with B. He's acting insane right now and the horses are back. No one has been hurt so I don't understand his reaction. And he flat-out won't talk to me other than to say not to worry about things.*

This time there was a pause from Valerie, then...

Valerie: *Maybe it's not about the horses.*

Burner phone (assumed Mila Kingston): *Huh? Then what's it about?*

Valerie: *Not sure, but I agree with you that us being out here like this bothering your high-dollar guests is odd. I gotta get off my phone for a bit. I'll check in later.*

Cash pulled her back against his bare chest. "It is interesting, but there's nothing we can do right now. Skye's contacted Hazel who's said she'll get back to us. And Skye said she also might have a line with the DEA. She *also* told us to sit tight. They're sending the jet in case we need to make a quick getaway."

Yeah, she knew all that, but she was very impatient on the best of days. Reese also didn't think anyone would be making a quick getaway with all that snow falling outside. But she kept that thought to herself. She punched the comforter underneath them for good measure before she slid her laptop to the bedside table. "I just don't like feeling useless. And it sounds like the detective knows something, or at least suspects something."

"Maybe she's in a weird position. This is a rural area. She could just be trying to do her job without making waves. And if she only suspects something's going on...there's not a lot she can do without losing her job or putting herself in danger. We don't know her situation."

Reese leaned back against Cash, savored the feel of his big arm wrapping around her. "Yeah, I know."

He nibbled on her earlobe for a moment, but paused when there was a loud bang downstairs. He cursed under his breath. "Ten bucks says it's that aggressive Detective Conroy."

"Not gonna take that bet," she muttered as she sat up and reached for her clothes.

"I'll grab the door. You can stay here."

She nodded, but tugged on jeans and a sweater anyway as Cash strode from the room. He snagged a pair of jeans from the floor on his way out and tugged them on, hiding that gorgeous ass as he disappeared out the door.

She automatically sighed as he covered up, but it was for the best. Whatever was going on, they were going to need to face it with clothing on. Once she was fully dressed, she headed downstairs to find that yep, Detective Conroy was there, his expression surly as he stood right in the doorway.

*Letting all the cold air in. Jackass.*

Cash turned as she entered the room, his green eyes landing on her mouth for a moment, before a serious expression slid into place. "There's been a murder."

She froze. "What?"

"Bode, Rae's husband was just found."

She blinked in surprise. "Oh my god. What happened? Was she hurt too?" She looked at the detective, and Cash turned back to him as well.

The detective eyed her for a moment, then stepped away. "I'm not here to answer questions. Meet at the main gathering area in the next five minutes. We need to talk to everyone." Then he turned and stalked off without another word, his boots stomping across the deck as he left.

Cash's eyebrows raised as he shut the door behind him. "This is definitely strange."

"Yeah, no kidding." She shot off a group text to Skye and Elijah while Cash ran upstairs to grab more clothes. She figured Skye could just loop Gage in if needed. She put her socks and shoes on by the door while she waited, then slid her jacket on as Cash reached her, fully dressed except for his boots.

Without a word, he slid her faux engagement ring on her bare finger before handing her the thick gloves and toque she'd left upstairs.

She ordered herself not to look at the ring as she slipped her gloves on. AKA, stare at it with stars in her eyes. *Jeez.* They were undercover, and sure things had definitely changed between them after the last few hours, but marriage? That was a whole other beast.

But she really, really liked that he kept putting the ring back on her even as she told herself not to read into things.

## Chapter 25

Cash tucked his phone and bear spray under his jacket as he headed out with Reese. Because his instinct that shit was about to go sideways was pinging out of control right now. Bode Brown had been murdered? Right after Kingston had murdered someone? Seriously, what the hell was going on?

The two murders could have nothing to do with one another, but right now it felt like they were sitting on a powder keg. And they couldn't reach out to local law enforcement about what they knew because they had no one to trust nearby. If anything, it seemed the cops were here to do Kingston's bidding. And now they were supposed to somehow trust these detectives to handle a murder? The same department that had brushed off Joelle's concerns about her friend being missing.

*Nope.*

As they approached the fire pit, he recognized most of the faces, including his ex, who he scanned over quickly. Everyone was gathered around, some sitting huddled together, others standing in clear annoyance, but unlike the last couple days there was no bar open and no smiling faces. Everyone looked sleep deprived and pissed off to be out in the freezing cold before the sun was even up. He didn't see Rowan or Adalyn, however.

Cash noticed that Ben Kingston was suspiciously gone, but Mila was there with Detective Lippman, looking nothing like the polished woman who'd first welcomed them to the resort. No big smile and styled hair. Her hair was pulled up into a messy ponytail and he didn't think she'd put on much makeup. She was a striking woman regardless, but she was the type who didn't go out unpolished.

"Thank you, everyone, for gathering together here," Mila Kingston said.

"Not like we had a choice," a man he vaguely recognized grumbled from his spot right in front of the fire.

"No, you don't." Detective Conroy stepped up, all aggression and obnoxiousness. "Because someone was murdered. We're going to need to talk to everyone here about their alibis and we're going to be searching the cabins."

Cash frowned at that.

"Why are you searching our cabins?" Isabella called out in that familiar, haughty tone he now loathed.

He wasn't sure how he'd ever fallen for her. No, that wasn't true. He *hadn't* fallen for her. He'd fallen for the show she put on, not the real her. Which was why it hadn't taken a minute to get over her—because what they'd had, had never been real.

"I don't want someone pawing through my things," she continued.

"And where's the medical examiner?" Cash called out. Because so far, he'd only seen police trucks.

Valerie stepped up when it looked as if Conroy was about to blow his top. "No one is going to paw through anyone's things. We're simply going to be looking at various shoes to see if they match up with the area around the crime scene. This should be quick and easy for everyone."

Reese handed Cash her phone, angling it so no one else could see it. They were standing behind two couples sitting on the benches and no one was behind them, but he understood why she wanted privacy when he looked at the screen. Rae was in Ben Kingston's office, sitting across from Ben and a large man in a sheriff's uniform. She was crying and...yeah, he didn't like this at all.

"I'm going to go interrupt whatever this is," he murmured to Reese. "Can you get loud?"

She snorted softly. "Oh yeah."

She moved around the circle, closer to the front where the detectives and Mila Kingston were trying to keep everyone calm. Well, Detective Lippman was. The other guy was clearly just a dick.

"No one has answered where the M.E. is. And where is Bode Brown's wife, Rae? Is she okay? I don't mind someone going through my cabin—I know that we don't have to give permission since we don't own them—but I don't appreciate the way we're being treated! No one has offered us food or drinks or anything. And you, *sir*, are just plain rude! You've barged in to all our cabins…"

Cash bit back laughter as he ducked behind the bar and made his way down one of the snow-covered paths as Reese raised her voice again, saying something about "stop treating us like criminals" in a snooty voice. Now, that haughty tone? Oh, he liked that one. But he shelved that thought as he approached the small office building.

He didn't bother knocking, just barged into the little lobby, then headed straight back to the office where Rae was currently crying in her chair while the two much larger men glowered at her.

Yeah, this was a bunch of bullshit.

"Who the hell are you?" The large man, who he now realized was the actual sheriff, now that he saw him up close, demanded.

"Ah, this is Cash Pierce." Ben's tone was a lot more civil. "We're in the middle of something right now."

"Oh, I see that. Mrs. Brown's husband was just murdered and instead of offering her comfort, two men are currently harassing her without any video cameras or witnesses present."

"Now see here—" The sheriff jumped to his feet.

"No, *you* see here," Cash snapped. "She's an American citizen and has certain rights that you're trampling all over. Is she under arrest?"

Ben shook his head, holding out a hand to still the sheriff. "No, we're just asking some questions—"

"Oh, the sheriff and a *civilian* are asking her some questions." He made a scoffing sound. "If she's not under arrest, is she allowed to walk out of here? And where the hell is the M.E.? Because from what I've heard so far, all you have is an alleged murder victim and instead of handling things properly, you're wrangling his new *widow* in here without a lawyer—"

"She didn't ask for a lawyer," the sheriff murmured.

"Do you want a lawyer?" Cash looked at the sniffling, red-eyed woman.

"I don't know. Maybe? I just...I'm so cold." She wrapped her arms around herself as she trembled slightly.

Oh he wanted to knock Kingston's head off right about now.

"Jesus Christ, you two should be ashamed of yourselves. She's been traumatized and instead of treating her like a human, you're in here grilling her. Unless either of you object, I'm going to take her out and get some tea and a thicker coat." He shook his head in disgust.

The sheriff actually looked ashamed as he cleared his throat. "That's...that's a good idea. And the M.E. is on the way. She had to switch vehicles because of all the snow so she's simply delayed."

Ben Kingston looked pissed, but didn't say a word.

And Cash gave exactly zero fucks. He'd learned in business long ago that if you took over like a bulldozer, about seventy-five percent of the time, people went along with you. Especially when you had money.

On the way out, he grabbed a coat hanging by the door, not caring who it belonged to, and handed it to her. "Just put this one for right now, at least until you get back to your cabin." As he stepped outside with Rae, he patted her gently on the back. "I'm really sorry about your husband."

"I didn't kill him," she blurted, looking up at him with wide, tear-filled eyes. "I didn't even know he'd been killed until..." She sucked in a ragged breath. "Until the sheriff showed up at my cabin. Bode never came back last night and I thought he must have been sleeping it off in a new cabin or—" She straightened at the sound of gunfire.

*What. The. Hell.*

Cash recognized the sound of automatic weapons. Multiple weapons. Oh god, *Reese.*

He grasped Rae's upper arm and tugged when she just stood there in shock, frowning. "Come on. I need to get you somewhere safe."

She seemed to jerk out of her haze and fell in step with him.

The gunfire was coming from the direction of where everyone was so he tugged her around the office building then pointed to the woods. It was still dark out, but the sun would be up in about half an hour. "Run to that tree line and hide. Go deep enough that no one will see you. Stay hidden until I come get you."

"What about you—"

"Go," he snapped, giving her a little push. "Run, now!"

Eyes wide, she nodded. "Stay safe," she whispered, racing for the line of snow-capped trees.

He eased back around the side of the office building as his phone buzzed. He slid his earpiece in. "Skye, I can't talk right now. We're dealing with a situation." And he had to get to Reese before his heart beat right out of his chest. She was smart and capable, but that wouldn't outrun a bullet. He shoved back the fear that wanted to drown him as he hurried back to the office and up a short set of stairs.

He didn't see anyone else, then nearly ran into the sheriff and Ben who were opening the door.

"Sheriff," he said, pushing the other man back inside. "Multiple shots fired," he told them, aware that Skye could hear everything. "No visual yet. But I need a weapon. I was a Night Stalker. Army. And we're dealing with multiple shooters."

Ben stared wide-eyed, but the sheriff kept it together, nodded once.

Even though his instinct was to race to where Reese was, he couldn't show up unarmed. And his bear spray wouldn't do much against bullets. So he was forcing himself to be patient and fall back on his army training.

"Here." The sheriff pulled out a backup pistol from his ankle, then nodded at what Cash had assumed was a supply closet. "Ben's got a couple rifles. Sometimes we deal with bears and mountain lions. Where's the woman?"

"I sent her to the trees to hide out. She should be safe."

"It's a group of Albanians," Skye said into Cash's ear, her tone low. "You don't have to say anything, but I'm giving you the rundown. My DEA contact got back to me. Turns out Kingston murdered the nephew of the leader of a very dangerous crew. Clearly he had no idea. They're out for blood. My contact got word that they were going to hit the wellness center from an informant only ten minutes ago. I was calling to warn you to get everyone to safety."

"We need to call for backup," Ben was saying to the sheriff.

"We're the backup, Ben," the sheriff snapped as he started pulling out rifles and boxes of ammo. "It's gonna take at least an hour for anyone to get here in this weather. Call the station and tell them what's going on."

"I heard someone shout something," Cash said, lying. "Sounded Albanian. You know what this is about?" he asked Ben as he took one of the rifles, slung it over his shoulder.

Ben shook his head, but yep, the guy was lying. Cash could see it clearly on his face. Didn't matter now.

"Stay here and hunker down after you call in for backup," Cash growled. He might not like the guy, but he wanted him to go to jail. To pay for his crimes. Death would be way too easy for Kingston. Then he turned to the sheriff who had a rifle slung over his shoulder as well, his pistol in hand. "We need to lure the gunmen away from everyone, to isolate them. The goal is to save everyone."

The man nodded, his expression grim. "I should be telling you to stay put."

"My soon to be wife is out there and I have training. I'm not staying anywhere." He shoved boxes of ammo in both pockets. "If you can make it to the stables, release the horses. As far as I know, another one of the guests here is military trained as well." And so was Adalyn, but he wasn't going to get into that. Wasn't going to give away all his secrets.

The sheriff looked as if he wanted to argue, and hell, Cash *was* just taking over, but someone had to. "Okay. Watch your six."

They hurried out the door into an eerie silence. The fact that the gunfire had been a short burst was the only thing keeping him sane right now. He was hoping it had simply been a warning shot to keep people corralled.

"You still there?" he murmured as he hurried across the bank of snow, racing toward one of the bigger buildings that housed the dining hall and kitchen.

"I'm here." Skye's voice was tense, but calm as always. "I've texted the others but haven't heard back. We're en route on the jet but with the stupid snow I'm not sure if we'll be able to land at the airport." She let out a savage curse. "They're trying to divert us."

"It's fine," he murmured as he flattened his back to the dining hall. He could hear a faint murmur of sound, maybe boots. "Going silent." He pitched his voice so low he almost couldn't hear himself as he swept around the corner, weapon up.

And found Adalyn standing above a man out cold in the snow, blood flowing from the side of the guy's head.

"Reese is okay," she whispered. "Sitting with a group of people in front of the fire. No one's been shot that I can tell. The volley of gunfire was just a show, I believe."

And just like that he could take in a full breath for the first time in four minutes.

The longest four minutes of his entire life. Of any lifetime he'd ever lived. She was okay. He needed eyes on her, but he could actually breathe now.

Crouching down, Adalyn started searching the guy while Cash kept his weapon up and ready to take down anyone who approached. He didn't like being exposed like this, even with the building giving them cover. "Where's Rowan?"

"Not sure. I was at the gym working out because I couldn't sleep. Heard an automatic weapon and jumped into action. What the hell is going on?" She tucked a pistol into the back of her pants, then palmed the other like a pro.

"The guy Ben killed is related to the Albanian mob. Or something to that effect. I'm on with Skye." He pointed to his ear.

Adalyn simply nodded as she retrieved a pistol from the fallen guy. Then she stood.

"We've got maybe twenty more minutes before the sun is up." He kept his voice low as he leaned in. "Let's go get our people." And by people, he meant Reese. Because at the moment, she was all he cared about.

# Chapter 26

Oh, they were in a shitstorm now. Reese eyed the four men wearing balaclavas and carrying MAC-10s. Three of the four men had suppressors, but one didn't. The one who'd shot off his weapon like a deranged lunatic and shouted at everyone to stay where they were.

He wasn't deranged, however. No, he was clearly the one in charge. He stood by the fire pit, his weapon at ease while the other three kept theirs trained on the trembling crowd. She counted about twenty guests total, so about ten to fifteen people were missing. Rowan, Adalyn and thankfully Cash were nowhere to be seen. Neither was Ben Kingston or a handful of employees.

The two detectives looked fit to be tied, but had thankfully surrendered their weapons without getting into a gun battle and were currently sitting on the ground with their hands on their heads as ordered. Because their two pistols against MAC-10s... It would have been a bloodbath with no winners. And these men were wearing balaclavas, which was a pro as far as she was concerned—they wanted to hide their faces which meant they might not plan on killing everyone. Fingers crossed.

The rest of the guests were all sitting looking a little shell shocked, though a handful just looked angry. Yeah, she felt that to her core as well.

"I'm going to make this easy on everyone," the leader said as he spun in a slow circle, looking at everyone. The crackling fire pit cast shadows on his balaclava, making his eyes look sunken in. Really selling that villain thing well.

"We are here for Ben Kingston. As soon as we have him, we'll leave. So. Where is he?" The man spun, whipped his weapon up so fast she barely saw the movement before he trained it right on Mila Kingston.

"I don't know," she whispered.

The man cocked his head to the side. "Wrong answer."

"Wait!" Reese called out, unable to stop herself. "I saw him headed to the stables. He's probably hiding now because he's a coward. But I have something you want. Proof that he's a murderer."

Reese felt all eyes on her, but the only person she focused on was the nameless leader with the dark, terrifying eyes. She resisted the urge to swallow hard even as her heart beat an erratic thump against her chest. She was already standing, but had to look up at him as he approached. She blinked against a couple snowflakes that hit her face.

"Who are you?"

"My name is Reese. I'm an investigator. I was hired to look into Mr. Kingston." As soon as the armed men had shown up, bleeding out of the shadows like a walking nightmare, she'd tossed her phone behind one of the benches. It was currently tucked between a giant blue planter and the bench. Hopefully the bench would protect it from the little snowfalls in the air, softly coating everyone.

The man blinked and she knew she'd surprised him. A small frown tugged at his already tight mouth. He tapped his ear once, then spoke quietly to someone in what was definitely a Slavic language. He paused, then looked at her. "What kind of proof?"

"A recording of him...shooting someone. When I followed him, I thought he was meeting up with a lover. He's cheated on his wife multiple times." She blended the truth and fiction, knowing it would help sell her story. "Instead, he met with two men on an ATV, both wearing dark hooded jackets. I couldn't see faces, but he shot one and then he and the other guy exchanged duffel bags. I got the murder on video and I pinned the location to mark where the body was."

There were a couple gasps from guests, but they were all short lived. And she didn't look away from the leader to see anyone's reaction. The only person she was concerned about was him anyway.

Another blink, but then his gaze turned calculating, disbelieving. "Why not call the cops? Isn't that what law-abiding citizens do?" There was a sneer in his voice as he shifted his gun slightly.

"I wasn't sure who I could trust. As part of my investigation, I looked hard at Kingston's financials and he's donated a lot to the local sheriff's re-election campaign. I reached out to the Feds only a few hours ago. I was just waiting for a call back."

There was a long pause, then he said something in a foreign language again, definitely talking to his boss, given the deferential tone. Then he looked at one of his men, said, "Stables. Now." Then he looked back at her. "I want to see this proof."

She kept her hands up, her heart still pounding in her ears. "It's at my cabin. We can go get it or I can tell you where it is and you can get it."

"Come with me." He turned to the other two men, shouted an order in that same language, then motioned at her with his weapon.

Once they were out of earshot of the others, well onto the walkway toward the cabin, he angled his weapon down and pulled out a cigarette, lit it up. "Who hired you? The wife?"

"I don't know. The way it works is anonymous."

"Anonymous?" He shot her a dark look, as if he knew she was lying.

She cleared her throat. "My work isn't exactly...*legal*." Again, she blended truth and fiction. "I work with a collective of other hackers and investigators and we take anonymous jobs for the right price. But yeah, if I had to guess, it was the wife. They've got a prenup that says if he cheats, well, he's screwed." Reese had no idea if it was true or not but played up this angle because it was believable.

"Ah." He nodded, as if this made complete sense. "My boss works with hackers too. Maybe if you play your cards right, he'll hire you."

She snorted. "Yeah, if you don't shoot me."

He barked out a laugh. "We're not here to kill anyone."

Well, except Ben Kingston.

As if he read her mind, he shook his head. "We're just retrieving him."

She wasn't sure if she believed him or not, but she motioned toward the cabin she'd been sharing with Cash. The sky was lightening every second that passed, a wash of oranges painting the east. And she almost swore she saw a hint of movement by the side of the house. "This is me," she murmured even as hope flared inside her that they weren't alone.

After tossing his cigarette butt into the snow, he held his weapon on her as he ordered her to open the door. And as they stepped inside, she winced because one of Cash's sweaters was tossed onto the nearest couch and a pair of his boots were by the door, next to another pair of hers.

The gunman noticed the shoes immediately, shoved the weapon in her face.

For a long moment, all she could do was stare down the barrel and try not to pee herself. She kept her hands up and forced herself not to stare into the abyss of her looming death. Instead she looked at the man. "What are you doing?" she demanded, annoyed with herself when her voice shook.

"You're not working alone."

"Yeah, I know. This place is for couples so I'm here undercover with a partner."

"Where is he?" His gaze left her face, but his weapon sure didn't as he visually scanned the living room and connected kitchen.

"Back with everyone else. I don't know why you're so angry. He was standing right next to me." *Lie.* But she didn't think he'd been paying attention. "I haven't said one lie to you. And I'm giving you proof that Ben Kingston is a murderer."

The man eyed her for a long moment, then lowered the weapon. Slightly. Instead of being trained on her face, it was now on her chest. *Just great.* If he put too much pressure on the trigger, he'd blow a hole through her chest instead of taking her head off. "Where's the proof?"

"How do I know you won't kill me once I give it to you?"

"You don't."

*Okay, then.* She kept her hands raised and ignored a hint of movement she saw by the window. Yep, she hadn't imagined that at all. "I have the video saved on a USB device. It's upstairs."

He motioned with his weapon in response so she turned and headed to the stairs, half expecting a bullet in her head as she ascended. Once in the bedroom, she pointed at the bathroom. "It's in with my toiletries." She had everything backed up and her crew already had copies in the file for this job, but she still clung to old habits. She kept backups for her backups. And right about now she was glad because she wasn't giving this asshole access to her files.

"Slowly." He pointed with the weapon so she kept one hand up and opened the bathroom door.

Still keeping one hand up, she reached into her makeup bag with the other and pulled out a dark blue USB, held it out.

He quickly palmed it, then motioned for her to head back out. "It's clear that your partner is a man. And it's clear that the two of you are sleeping together. I find it pathetic that he let you go off alone with an armed man." His tone was derisive as they descended the stairs, but she ignored the man.

It wasn't like she could admit that Cash hadn't been there at all.

"I think I'll have words with him when we return."

She bit back the snarky response on the tip of her tongue. Right now she had to play it smart and stay alive long enough for Cash to kick this guy's ass. Because she had no doubt he would back her up. This might be their first job together, but he had her six. Always.

And that thought was humbling.

Because he'd put himself out there from the beginning, had shown her exactly who he was. No pretense. And she'd been so damn determined to keep walls up to avoid getting hurt. *Well look at me now*, she growled silently to herself. *What a fool I've been.*

As they reached the end of the hallway that led to the living room and kitchen area, the man's radio crackled. She stepped through the opening as the man answered.

And suddenly Cash was there, flattened against the wall next to the hallway. He grabbed the weapon, shoved it upward as he attacked.

She ducked, trying to get out of the way as he slammed the guy into the wall. The gun clattered to the floor between them as they exchanged fast, hard blows.

But this man was clearly trained.

She sprinted to the kitchen, pulled out a huge knife from the butcher block.

Cash blocked what would have been a strike to the head as he kicked out at the fallen MAC-10.

As he struck out at the masked man, the other man lashed out, grazing Cash's thigh as he dodged backward.

Then in a surprise move, the man threw his entire body at Cash, tackling him into the coffee table. Wood and glass splintered and shattered as the two men tumbled to the ground. And that was when she saw the glint under the lighting.

"He's got a knife!" she shouted as she dove for the MAC-10, scooped it up.

She aimed upward, pulled the trigger once, setting off a barrage of gunfire. Plaster rained down on the men and they both froze.

The masked man held his hands up as he turned to face Reese. "My men will be on the way now."

"I could just shoot you then, couldn't I?" she snapped even as Cash slammed something hard down on the back of the guy's head.

He crumpled, falling against the broken glass and wood with a heavy thud.

"Unless you want to get in a gun battle, we've gotta get out of here," Cash said. "Out the front door."

She raced out the front door with Cash right as she heard the back door slam open.

## Chapter 27

Finally armed with a blade, Rowan eased out of the storage room in the stables and turned, his sickle in hand. Then he froze at the sound of a weapon being cocked to his left. *Hell.* And he'd been so careful.

"Set the weapon down and slowly turn toward me," a slightly accented voice spoke from the left.

A couple horses whinnied in their stables and a sharp wind whistled through the barn as Rowan set the sickle against the half-open door. He raised both hands before slowly turning toward the voice. A masked man had a MAC-10 trained right on his chest.

"Who are you and what are you doing out here?" the man demanded.

"Ah, I'm a guest here. Name's Rick. Heard the gunfire, wanted to protect myself. I've got money in my cabin. And a nice Rolex as well." He slowly reached over with one hand and pushed a sleeve up to show it. "Oh, I've also got some Tylenol for that headache."

The man's head tilted to the side slightly as he eyed him in confusion.

Rowan didn't wince as Adalyn slammed a two-by-four across the back of the guy's head. But he did smile.

"Jesus, you're quiet," he murmured. "I could see you sneaking up on him but couldn't hear you."

She simply shoved a pistol at him. "This'll be better than that sickle. Though not as cool." Then she quickly patted the guy down as he plucked up the MAC-10. "Cash just contacted me," she continued. "He and Reese are fine for now. They're hiding out in one of the cabins after they took out one of the guys. Both have weapons, but she doesn't have a phone."

"Did they kill the guy?" Rowan glanced around the stables, the back of his neck itching. A couple horses stomped in annoyance, not liking the situation either. He didn't like feeling so exposed, so many unknowns. Shit had blown up with no warning in the form of a bunch of armed men. And he had no clue if they were all trigger-happy or open to negotiation. The only thing he knew from Skye was that the men here were Albanians—courtesy of Ben Kingston's murderous stupidity.

"No. Just knocked him out. So far no one's been killed. I knocked out one of their guys—well, two now. But I didn't have time to secure him."

Rowan ducked back into the storage shed and grabbed a bundle of rope. "We can toss this one in one of the empty stalls."

Adalyn nodded, her weapon up as he got to work hog-tying the guy. He wasn't getting out of this without help.

At the sound of the heavy door rolling open, Rowan scooped up the MAC-10, aimed it at the opening as Adalyn did the same.

A man in a sheriff's uniform—he recognized the guy from their intel file. Sheriff Wicker and Ben Kingston stepped into the stable. The sheriff had his pistol up as well but Ben hadn't even pulled his rifle around.

"We're guests and on your side," Adalyn said as she held her weapon down by her thigh.

Rowan kept his up because (a) it was in his nature and (b) he didn't trust either of these two assholes.

"They are guests," Ben said quietly, shutting the door behind the two of them, still not reaching for his rifle.

The sheriff lowered his weapon, but didn't sheath it as he strode toward them, nodding at the now slightly groaning guy. "We need to find out who these guys are and what they want."

Oh, Rowan knew what the gunmen wanted and he couldn't tell if the sheriff was just a damn good actor or if he really didn't know. Because the sheriff was in on the drug running with Kingston. He had to be. It was the only thing that made sense, especially considering how much Ben had donated to the guy's re-election fund. He was paying him off in a very legal way that wouldn't be questioned.

"Our friends are here," Adalyn said to the sheriff. "So don't shoot."

They all looked as the door creaked open again and Cash and Reese hurried in.

The sheriff seemed to relax when he spotted Cash, nodded at him. "I just got here. Haven't had a chance to unleash the horses as a distraction."

"That's fine," Cash said, giving Rowan a subtle chin jerk.

Rowan wasn't sure what that was about until Cash continued.

"We've got a new plan." He held his weapon on Ben Kingston. "We're going to hand this bastard over to the Albanians."

# Chapter 28

"What the hell are you doing?" The sheriff looked at Cash in shock.

But Cash kept his pistol trained on Ben Kingston as Reese relieved him of his weapon.

"I'll take yours." Adalyn trained her pistol on the sheriff, her expression hard.

The man looked at all of them, including Rowan, who simply shrugged.

"What are you doing? We need to hunker down until backup arrives," Ben Kingston snapped even as Reese set his rifle in the storage room.

"Oh we're going to stop these guys," Cash said. "And since it's Ben's fault that they're all here, we're going to trade his life for all of ours. He killed some Albanian mob boss's nephew or something. Isn't that right?" Cash looked at Ben, eyebrows raised.

"Oh, you stupid son of a bitch," the sheriff muttered, rubbing a hand over his face.

"It was self-defense!" Kingston snapped.

"Ah, no. No, it wasn't." Reese shook her head, her expression dry. "I've got it on video. Not only that, he killed Aubry Boyle, then dumped her on his property. Tried to make it look like she quit, moved back home, but we've got a witness who saw you emptying out her cabin in the middle of the night. And a witness who saw you two arguing about your relationship."

The last part wasn't true about the arguing but Cash knew that his woman was trying to set the tone, to get this asshole to fully confess.

"Stupid, stupid," the sheriff snarled, ignoring all of them as he glared at Kingston. "I always knew your dick would get us in trouble. But you killed that innocent girl? And one of the Albanians? What the hell is wrong with you."

In that moment, Ben Kingston's civilized mask slid away as he practically bared his teeth at the sheriff. "The dumb bitch was pregnant! She was going to tell Mila, ruin everything we've built. But it was self-defense. She attacked me first."

"She was a hundred and ten pounds." The sheriff growled at him in horror, doing all the work for them by pulling out a confession.

"Fuck you! And you know what, you can't make me—"

Cash aimed his weapon right at Kingston's face as the others did the same. "Want to try that again?" His question was rhetorical, but he liked the fear, the dawning of reality that was spreading across the asshole's face. Cash flicked a glance at Rowan. "Got more of that rope?"

Wordlessly Rowan nodded and yanked Kingston's hands behind his back. To Cash's surprise, the other man didn't struggle as Rowan bound his wrists tight.

"Why'd you kill the man the other night?" Cash asked even as Reese grabbed a rag from the storage room.

"None of your business," Ben snarled. "But the bastard deserved it."

Yeah, here was the real Ben Kingston. The murdering, greedy asshole.

Rowan took the rag that Reese handed him and shoved it over the guy's mouth. Now, Kingston did start to struggle.

"Stop it or I'll hog-tie you like that asshole." Cash nodded at the bound man on the ground.

The Albanian was awake now, but hadn't said anything. He was simply watching them with a glare.

"So what's the plan?" Rowan asked, looking between Cash and Reese.

"First I'm going to need to cuff you, sheriff." Cash gave the man an apologetic look. It was clear that he hadn't been involved in the murders. "I know you were involved in running drugs and I flat-out don't trust you."

The man's expression darkened, but he finally nodded and put his hands behind his back in resignation.

Moving quickly, Cash cuffed him, then secured him to one of the open shelves in the storage room and shut the door. The guy might escape but it would take time. And they would hopefully have the situation under control by then.

"We're all going to have to work together for this." And he needed to tell them the plan away from their hostage. "Come on." He motioned for the others to follow him down to one of the empty stalls.

Time was running out and they needed to ensure everyone made it out of here alive before it was too late.

Once they'd gone over everything, he and Rowan stalked back to their hostage, untied him enough so that he could stand while the women headed in the other direction loaded for metaphorical bear. This was the only part of the plan Cash hated—being separated from Reese.

But he trusted her to have his back.

Cash held out the man's radio. "You're going to call your boss and set up a meeting."

The man spit on the ground.

Cash simply sighed, ignored it. "Now, you're going to call your boss and tell him the truth. That we haven't hurt you and we simply want to exchange you and Kingston for all the innocent people here. We're not law enforcement and we don't want any bloodshed. You can walk away today."

The man looked between him and Rowan, made a scoffing sound. "Seriously?"

"We don't care about Kingston. We were hired for a job and we've done it. We just want to go home. You can call your boss or I can do it myself."

The man looked hard at both of them, then finally nodded. "Fine."

"In English," Cash said as he held up the radio. "And if you try anything stupid, I'll shoot you in the knee."

# Chapter 29

"I'd like to say for the record that I don't like this plan," Reese grumbled over the earpiece.

"Too bad." Cash had needed her to stay back and make sure the hostages were actually released while they met with the gunmen in the woods.

The sun had finally crested the sky, revealing a winter wonderland of quiet and unparalleled beauty.

Cash kept his weapon trained on the back of the Albanian, who'd they'd half untied so he could walk/shuffle along with them. Adalyn had recognized some of the man's tattoos and told them they needed to be very careful with this prisoner. "Stop," he ordered the man whose hands were bound behind his back, his feet bound with two loops, but with a knot in the middle attached to both so he could only take small steps.

They hadn't bothered with Kingston's legs since he had zero training. Though Cash certainly wouldn't underestimate the asshole enough to untie him. Not when he'd admitted to coldly killing a pregnant woman.

Rowan kept his weapon on Kingston as they strode toward the meeting place. The man Cash had knocked out earlier was stalking toward them through the snow, his balaclava back on.

Okay, so maybe they'd all get out of this relatively unscathed. If he'd put it back on, hopefully the guy hadn't shown his face to any of the hostages. Unfortunately there was no telling because he didn't have enough intel.

The man ripped his mask off when he was about twenty yards from the four of them. "You've got a lot of stones."

"So I've been told. And before any of your men get trigger-happy, you might want to let them know that you're in the crosshairs of a very skilled sniper."

The man's eyes narrowed. "I'm here alone, as you can see."

"He's got three guys that I can see," Adalyn's voice came through the earpiece clearly. "They're fanning out."

"Oooh, I thought we were going to be honest with each other." He shook his head, then murmured, "Give him a warning."

Adalyn pulled the trigger from her hiding spot in the trees, sending up a blast of snow two feet from the man's boots.

To his credit, he didn't jump, but Cash saw his body language change from secure to on-alert.

"Tell your men to hold where they are. Or the next one won't miss."

"Have they hurt you?" the leader called out.

"No. And they just cuffed the sheriff," their prisoner answered. "They're not law enforcement. Maybe they were at one point," he said, giving Rowan a sideways glance. "But they're not now."

Rowan just grinned at the guy, though it was more of a baring of teeth.

"So how do you want to do this?" the man said, now looking at Cash.

"It's going to be an even trade. You get your man here back, along with Ben Kingston, and you let the hostages go. We've got someone in place to confirm that they've all been released. Once you do that, you get these two. And to show that I'm extra grateful for your cooperation..." Cash grinned. "You get your drugs too."

"Drugs?"

"Yep. We stole them from Kingston here last night. Take them or leave them. I don't care."

"Yousonofabish," Kingston snarled around his gag and turned to lunge at Cash, but Rowan kicked the back of his knees, sending him sprawling into the snow.

Then Rowan planted a big boot on his back. "Stay still or you'll regret it."

The man was silent for a long moment, then he pulled out his radio, spoke quietly into it.

"The two men are motioning for the hostages to get up," Reese said through the earpiece.

"Tell your guys to send the hostages to ATVs. And tell them to ride off on the nearest trail." It was the best way for them to get distance between the gunmen.

The man gritted his teeth, then spoke into the radio again, repeating Cash's instructions.

"They're letting all of them go except the two cops."

"Let the detectives go too."

"No. They're my insurance."

"Insurance from what? We're giving you a good deal where everyone wins. Unless you're going to let your ego get in the way. Because if you kill two cops, you're dumber than I thought."

The man glared at Cash, then spoke quietly to someone, likely into an earpiece because he wasn't holding his radio up. Then he looked back up. "If you try to double-cross us—"

"I don't give a crap about you or your operations. My only priority is getting innocent people to safety. That's it. And you can take this murdering piece of shit with you." He nodded once at Kingston, who was still splayed in the snow, hands bound behind his back.

"Fine, but they're not taking their weapons."

"Of course not."

"Okay, the detectives are being released too. They're leaving with the other hostages. I can't see the ATVs but I can hear the engines starting up," Reese said. "And the armed men are heading in the other direction, back the way we entered when we first got here. They must have vehicles waiting for them."

"Stay put," he murmured loud enough for only Reese. "Do not move from your spot until we're back there."

"I know," she said, shivering. "But it's freaking cold up on this roof."

"Yeah, yeah," Adalyn said over the comm. "I'm up a freaking tree right now freezing my tits off."

He bit back a smile at the two of them. Then he bent down and cut the rope on his prisoner. "You're good to go."

The man shot him a dark look over his shoulder, but stalked toward his boss as Rowan tugged Kingston to his feet.

"Youcan'tdothis," he said around his gag.

"Oh, we can and we are. Did Aubry beg for her life while you were strangling her? I hope they give you as much mercy as you gave her."

"What about the drugs?" the man called out.

"Right underneath me," Cash said, stepping back. "Under the snow in a duffel." And he definitely wasn't digging it up for them.

"You want me to hold position?" Adalyn asked.

"No," he murmured, stepping away, not giving this guy his back. "Climb down. We all head out together."

He and Rowan hustled backward while the man ordered one of his men to start digging. As soon as they moved deeper into the forest and out of view, Adalyn dropped down in front of them. "They're gonna be pissed once they find out what's in store for them."

"That's a problem for future us. Let's get to Reese and the hostages." Before he lost his mind. Because he needed to hold Reese in his arms—and screw holding back anymore. She was his.

# Chapter 30

Reese pulled out her phone when it buzzed in her jacket pocket—and was glad that leaving it in the cold hadn't ruined it—as she jogged in the direction the rest of the hostages had gone. "Hey. Where are you?"

"Just landed on the highway," Skye said.

"Wait, can you repeat that?"

"Ah, long story. But I wanted to let you know that the DEA's RRT is in place. They're grabbing the Albanians when they exit the property."

Relief punched through her, then another surge immediately followed when she spotted Cash, Rowan and Adalyn racing toward her from the direction of the stables. She veered off course as she headed toward them. "They could kill Kingston in the vehicle."

"I know, but it's unlikely. Their boss, Dren Shehu, will want to have some fun with him for killing his nephew."

"You think this will fall back on us? Like blowback in the form of retribution?"

"I've got that covered."

"That's not an answer." *Skye*, she mouthed as she reached the others, a little out of breath but a lot excited to see them. She barely resisted the urge to throw herself into Cash's arms.

"I know. But we'll talk later. Get yourselves to cover. I'll see you soon." Then she disconnected.

"Wait..." *Damn it.* Reese shoved her phone back in her pocket. "Should we leave the sheriff where he is?"

"Yep." Cash pulled her into his arms into a big bear hug. "He's a problem for the DEA, not us."

And Reese didn't care that they had an audience. She grabbed his face and kissed him hard. She knew she'd surprised him by the public display, but he leaned into it for one long moment.

Then he pulled back and set her back on her feet. "We've got to get to the hostages, make sure everyone is accounted for."

Adalyn and Rowan nodded and the four of them hustled to where the others had escaped to.

"We've also got to find Rae," Cash murmured.

"Yeah. And figure out what happened to her husband," Reese added.

"I'm guessing that one of the Albanians killed him."

"You think?"

"Maybe. And maybe we'll never know." He shrugged, but she saw the hint of worry on his ridiculously handsome face as they reached the last ATV.

Adalyn jumped into the driver's seat before anyone else could. "Buckle up."

She tore out of the spot before Reese had actually secured her seat belt in the back, but Cash had a firm grip around her shoulder.

"You were pretty brave facing off with them," she said as she scooted as close as possible with the restraint.

The ATV had a windshield in front so the wind wasn't biting at least.

"Nah." He laid his head on hers. "I wasn't worried."

"Liar." She nudged him in the ribs. Or maybe he hadn't been worried. She sure had been. And being afraid for someone at work was normal to an extent, but this had been a different kind of fear. One she'd never experienced before. The fear of losing Cash had been all-consuming because if she'd lost him, it would have ripped out a part of her heart. And that was the kind of thing that could never be fixed.

It didn't matter if she tried to keep walls up or not at this point. She'd fallen for him harder than she ever could have imagined.

Leaning down, he murmured against her ear. "What's that expression?"

She smiled at him, wondering if he could see right through to her innermost thoughts. "Just glad we're all okay. Especially you." She squeezed his thigh to reiterate her point, then left her hand there. Because it didn't matter what the others thought—she didn't care.

She might not know what the hell she and Cash were, but she didn't give a fig what anyone thought of their relationship. And once they were back home…she wanted to actually define their relationship.

And maybe imagine a future with the two of them.

# Chapter 31

"I bet he flips on Kingston," Cash murmured to Reese as he watched a uniformed DEA agent put the cuffed sheriff in the back of one of their SUVs.

The last few hours had been a lot. The majority of guests were currently back in their cabins after answering questions from the Feds. He and Reese were in the main dining area, warm and toasty with a great view of what was going on outside in the freezing cold. The snow had picked up again, adding to everyone's misery. Though under other circumstances, he'd have loved it.

The Albanians were long gone, having been arrested along with Ben Kingston. Cash didn't know where they were being taken and he didn't care. They'd more than done their job.

"Probably not gonna matter either way, considering the recording we gave the DEA." Reese grinned, looking smug and a bit feral.

God, she was gorgeous like that. "Yeah, that confession is gold. And it's clear the sheriff wasn't involved in the murders."

Reese nudged him in the side. "Looks like someone's coming out."

Cash followed her line of sight to where Valerie was holding Mila Kingston close, cupping her cheeks tenderly. Mila leaned in and kissed her briefly before burying her face against the detective's neck.

"I hope they work out," Cash said.

Apparently Mila had known her husband was a dick, but hadn't realized the extent. She'd been satisfied to run a business with him since they hadn't shared a bedroom in years. They'd essentially been living separate lives and had fallen into a routine. Unfortunately for her, he'd been using their business to funnel drugs all along the Northeast and likely even farther.

"Me too." She leaned her head on his shoulder and he savored the feel of her against him, especially after the danger she'd been in before. He almost regretted not killing that guy who'd pulled a weapon on her, but things had worked out and they'd avoided bloodshed.

"Hey, you two." They both turned at the sound of Skye's voice. In all-white winter gear, she looked like she was ready to hit the slopes. Her auburn hair was pulled back in a braid, as per usual. "Our window is closing and we need to get the hell out of here. DEA's mostly done, though the RRT lead wants to talk to you, Cash. Can you guys pack up and be ready to roll in fifteen?"

"Oh, hell yeah." Reese nodded. "Cash, you talk to that guy and I'll pack for both of us." Then she paused, gave Skye a sly look. "Is the reason our window is closing because you landed in the middle of the highway?"

"It's not like I personally landed it, but yeah, the state police are pissed at us. I don't know why, not like anyone is out driving in this mess anyway. But they've got their panties all twisted up. Colt is currently smoothing things over, thankfully. But they've got some trucks out there clearing a path for us and we need to get gone fast."

"I'll pack like lightning." Reese grabbed Cash's hand, then tugged him down for a quick kiss before she hurried off.

Skye didn't look surprised by it and he knew the others hadn't said anything. They wouldn't have. "I hear you all worked well together. If it continues to work, I think you two should be paired up more often than not. Especially if you end up getting married. You'll be one of our best undercover couples because it'll be real."

Cash nodded, liking the sound of working with Reese. Of being with her all the time and making a difference. He'd been looking for something that felt right for as long as he could remember, always open to new adventures and job opportunities. He rarely said no if something was interesting work-wise. It was probably why he'd been so successful. And okay, he had a head for business. But he'd never felt the sense of rightness that he had with this job. He'd loved the army, but he'd never been able to choose what he wanted to do, how he wanted to help. Though he was grateful for the damn training. But this job felt like a calling, something he'd never get tired of.

"Oh, you didn't even balk at the M-word," Skye breathed out, her eyes slightly widening before she broke into a grin.

He simply grinned back, lifted a shoulder, not bothering to comment. "Who wanted to talk to me?"

"Come on." She led him outside to where a cluster of men and women were talking in front of a darkly tinted SUV. They all had on heavy blue jackets clearly emblazoned with *DEA* on the back. But one man wore fatigues and had various weapons strapped onto his body. "Give me a sec," she murmured, breaking off and striding toward the group.

Cash leaned against the railing of the small set of stairs, already counting down until they got home and could finally be alone and out of danger. There were still some loose ends, like who'd killed Bode Brown, but his wife wasn't under arrest and the DEA had tossed the murder investigation to a local FBI office. Whatever, wasn't his circus or his monkeys, but he'd already let Rae know that any lawyer she wanted would be on him. Because even if she had killed her husband, something told him the bastard had deserved it. But he'd seen the shock on her face; her grief and surprise had been too real. And the last thing he wanted was some innocent woman being railroaded because it was the easy solution.

"Thank you for talking to me," Commander Levine said upon greeting. "I know you guys are ready to get out of here."

"No problem. What do you need?"

"We arrested everyone in the two SUVs, including Kingston, but your number of shooters and mine aren't adding up. I just want to go over everyone you saw and talked to one more time. Just want to make sure my team has it right."

"Are you saying you're missing someone? Or someones?"

He shook his head. "Nope. Just want to do a double-check."

Frowning, Cash nodded and followed after the man as Skye hung back and started talking quietly to another uniformed agent. They stopped at one of the SUVs and he opened the passenger door, handed Cash a laptop.

"I only saw a couple faces," Cash said as he scanned the images on-screen. They were spread out like mugshots, four on top, four underneath, but of the eight on-screen, only two were actual mugshots. "But there were nine men that we counted. And the guy I spoke to isn't here."

"You're sure?"

"I got into hand-to-hand combat with the guy, then negotiated the exchange of the hostages for Kingston with him. I'm certain."

Commander Levine frowned then muttered to himself as he pulled up another screen. This time there were a lot more pictures. "These are all known members of this crew. Any of them look familiar?"

Cash used his finger to scroll the screen up, up— "There. That's him." He hovered his finger over an image of a man with dark hair, dark eyes, a couple tattoos peeking up from his shirt, and a hard expression. Alban Shehu.

The man let out another low curse, then whistled, gathering everyone's attention. "We've got a missing target," he called out in a booming voice. As he started barking orders about setting up roadblocks and looking into nearby farms, Skye strode up to him.

"Come on, this isn't our deal. Go grab Reese, I'll get Rowan and Adalyn. We're gone in seven minutes max. Don't make me leave you."

Cash wasn't sure if she was joking, but started jogging through the snow anyway.

When he stepped inside the cabin, he immediately knew something was wrong. Their coats were still hanging up, two pairs of shoes were by the door, and Reese's laptop was on the floor by the fireplace.

Heart racing, he sprinted upstairs only to find it empty. His instinct was to call out her name, but in case there was someone lying in wait, he was being as quiet as possible. When it was clear that the place was empty, he called Skye.

"Reese is missing and I think I know who took her."

# Chapter 32

"You better not be lying about this," the man growled, shoving his pistol into Reese's back again.

"I'm not lying." She'd told him about the pickup truck they had a couple miles away when it had been clear he wanted to use her as a hostage.

"That's what your boyfriend said and there was a DEA team waiting for me and my guys."

"Technically, he didn't lie—"

The man shoved her again.

*Okay, then.* She gritted her teeth as she hurried across the snow-packed trailway. The gunman had grabbed her as she'd been packing up. He'd changed clothes, looked like one of the guests now. And she could only wonder if he'd hurt someone to get those clothes. She hoped he'd simply stolen them. "How'd you get away?"

"No talking."

She hurried forward, pretty sure she'd avoided another "nudge" with his pistol.

To her surprise, he answered her question. "The whole trade was too easy so I said I was going to hang back and meet up with the others after I did a final sweep. Glad I did," he muttered more to himself.

"If you kill me—"

"I'm not going to kill you."

Said the man with a gun trained on her who'd abandoned his own men. The guy was a cockroach.

"Come on, pick up the pace." He shoved her again.

This time she stumbled and fell, spreading out dramatically in the snow. If Cash was going to find her—and she had faith that he would figure out where she'd gone—she was going to leave a big trail.

She cried out when he yanked her up by the arm. "If you keep pushing me, you're going to slow us down," she snapped as she dusted snow off her clothes. Ignoring the twinge of pain in her arm, she fell in step with him when he simply motioned with his pistol.

Man, she wished she was as trained as Cash. She'd always been satisfied with her role at Redemption Harbor Security, but if she survived this, she was going to get more self-defense training.

"You look a little murderous," he said all casual as he glanced down at her.

*Smug bastard.* "Well, I *am* contemplating your death."

Surprise flickered in his dark eyes, but he just continued stalking through the snow. "So why were you guys really here?"

She motioned to the trail they needed to take. "I wasn't lying about the reason. I didn't lie about...almost anything. The wife didn't hire us, but other than that, we were there to find a missing woman."

"Was she wealthy or something?"

"Why does that matter?"

He just lifted a shoulder, then paused, held a finger to his mouth. That was when she heard the sound of an ATV in the distance, and it was coming their way. "Go," he whispered, pointing into the woods.

The snow came up to right below her knees as she headed into the forest. It was thick with trees, though an ATV could manage to squeeze through in some places. Still, the hope that had been burning bright inside her dimmed.

"Oh shit." She stopped dead in her tracks, earned a shove but barely registered it as she stared at the tawny-colored beast about thirty feet away from them. Its amber eyes glinted in the sunlight and the mountain lion looked way too thin, her musculature far too defined and visible.

"Wh—" The man froze next to her, held up his weapon. "Shit," he muttered, clearly realizing that if he shot her, it would give away their location.

She took a step back.

"Don't move."

"You can shoot me, then. When faced with mountain lions you're supposed to walk away from them but not give them your back. And you're supposed to stand up straight, to look as big as possible. And make sure you maintain eye contact."

"How the hell do you know this?" he asked quietly as he stepped backward with her.

She made sure to remain behind him because the mountain lion was only about thirty feet from them, a beautiful, deadly beast against an equally beautiful backdrop of snow and thick trees. She could hear the engine of the ATV nearby, but it sounded as if it had gone past them. *Great.*

The big cat cocked its head slightly to the side as it stared at them. She forced herself to maintain eye contact.

"I read up on the wildlife in the area before coming here. This one shouldn't be this close to the resort, but it's clear she's hungry. Maybe has cubs to feed." Her ribs were visible, but she was still pure, raw strength as she took another step toward them.

Reese resisted the urge to run, but her blood rushed in her ears, a wild storm.

"Forget this, I'm getting out of here." His body language was vibrating as he took another step past her, going faster, faster.

"Don't run. It'll trigger her prey drive." Even more panic punched through her, because they were still way too close to the beast—who could jump up to forty-five feet. And even if she couldn't, she could easily chase them.

But the man turned and ran, his big legs eating up distance in the snow. Reese swore her heartbeat stopped as the cat pounced straight toward them in a fluid, deadly move. Reese dove for the snow, curling into a ball as the white-gray belly sailed over her with grace.

A short, muffled scream sounded, but was cut off when... She swallowed back bile as the cat looked directly at her, its mouth bloody. Reese didn't look at the savaged body or she'd lose what little breakfast she'd had. Somehow she held the cat's gaze until it looked away and started feeding.

She slapped a hand over her mouth and forced herself to go slowly as she continued backing away. Only once she had enough distance and was sure the cat wasn't paying attention to her did she pick up her pace.

She wasn't sure if the cat would come after her next, so as soon as she hit the trail she started running as fast as the snow would allow.

At the sound of an engine gaining on her, she turned and nearly wept when she saw Cash riding toward her, his expression dark and...terrified. He had a weapon held in one hand as he steered, looking around for her captor.

"He's dead!" she shouted as she raced toward him. "A mountain lion killed him," she rasped out, her entire body trembling as he pulled her into his arms. "I told him not to run, but he didn't listen." And he'd paid the price.

"Seriously?" He stared in shock even as he lifted her right onto the ATV, nudged her over to the passenger side.

"I wouldn't have believed it unless I saw it with my own eyes."

"How far's the body from here?"

She pointed behind her. "About fifty yards back, then head west straight into the forest."

He pulled out his phone and dropped a pin, then kicked the vehicle into drive. "The DEA can deal with him. I'm getting you the hell out of Montana and I don't think we're ever coming back."

Something about the way he said "we" broke every wall she'd ever tried to erect. Hot tears stung her eyes as she buried her face against his shoulder.

He cursed under his breath as he wrapped an arm around her. "You're okay. You're okay," he murmured, his voice a balm to her soul as they sped away from the carnage.

# CHAPTER 33

Cash scooped Reese into his arms, not planning to let her out of his sight for oh... how about ever.

"What are you doing?" Reese mumbled against Cash's neck.

"Just close your eyes." The jet had landed, and thankfully Skye had arranged for rides for all of them. Reese had fallen asleep almost as soon as they'd gotten on the plane and he wasn't letting her out of his sight anytime soon.

"Are we home?" she mumbled again, this time lifting her head up as they started to descend the boarding stairs.

"Almost."

Grumbling to herself, she buried her face against his shoulder and neck. He was grateful for the trust she was putting in him, because Reese from a week ago wouldn't have allowed anyone to carry her off a plane. Or hell, just take over like this.

"That's yours." Skye pointed to one of four identical SUVs. "I'll call you in the morning, we'll all meet up."

He simply nodded, watching as their driver opened the back door for them, then loaded up their bags. He'd forgotten about their bags, wondered who the hell had packed up for them. Because after finding Reese racing at him, her eyes wide with terror and then relief, everything was a blur.

The one thing he did remember was Skye telling the DEA commander to pound sand when he'd tried to hold them for more questioning. Her exact words had been, "You lost the guy, now he's been eaten by a mountain lion. Seems like the problem solved itself. We're leaving unless you plan on arresting us." And that had been that.

Oh, he was sure they'd have to answer more questions later, but for now, the DEA had just landed a big win. Everything else was a problem for the future, so he shut his eyes and held the woman he was a hundred percent sure he loved close as they headed home.

\*\*\*

Cash frowned at his phone screen when he saw Isabella's number on the caller ID. Reese was right, he should have just blocked her. Though he was tempted to reject the call, he answered, wondering if this was about what had happened at the wellness retreat. He hadn't talked to her since everything had blown up, though he had seen that she was okay, along with the other hostages. And he'd felt absolutely nothing when he'd seen her.

"Yeah?" he answered as he pressed start on his coffeepot.

Reese had been asleep since they'd arrived home and was still sleeping however many hours later. But the sun was up and he was pretty sure she'd wake up if he cooked bacon for her.

"Oh..." She cleared her throat. "I wasn't sure if you'd answer. Are you home now?"

"Yeah. What's up?" He peered in his fridge, frowned when he saw how little was in there. He really needed to go grocery shopping.

"We're home too. Managed to get out on a private plane. That was...intense, huh?"

"Uh, yeah."

She let out a sigh. "Look, I'm just going to say it. What you and your partner did was really brave. You guys saved us. If I'd known you were just undercover..."

She trailed off, then picked up again. "I miss you, Cash. I miss us. I know I screwed up, but I want a second chance."

Cash knew he should probably answer civilly, but he was over her bullshit. "I'm sure you want a second chance at my money, but nothing between Reese and me is fake. So, no thank you." He ended the call, then blocked her just like he should have done before.

"I take it that was Isabella." He turned at Reese's raspy voice.

Wearing one of his T-shirts, she yawned as she stepped into the kitchen, looking half asleep and good enough to eat. God, he'd missed her and they'd only been separated by one floor. Her jet-black hair was tousled and all he wanted to do was say screw the coffee and bacon and haul her back to bed. "Ah, yeah. I blocked her."

Her eyes widened and she looked more awake at that. "Hmm."

"What does that sound mean?"

"Just interesting, that's all." Her green eyes brightened when she looked behind him. "Did you make coffee?"

"It's still brewing and don't change the subject."

"I'm not changing anything. I just don't want to talk about your ex." She strode toward him, looking more and more awake with each step. "So did I sleep for an entire day or is it just Friday?"

"It's Wednesday. And we have to meet up with the others in a couple hours." He reached into his pocket, took her left-hand, and slid her not-so-fake engagement ring on her finger.

She blinked up at him. "We're not undercover anymore."

"Pretty sure I was never undercover when it came to you." No pretty sure about it.

She covered his mouth with her hand, her expression one he couldn't quite read. There was a little horror mixed in with longing. "Why do you always say the most perfect things!"

He nipped at her palm. "Why does that sound more like an accusation?"

"Because it is. You've made me completely fall for you!"

"Is that a bad thing?" He loosely held her hips as he pulled her closer. And that was when he realized she wasn't wearing any panties. Or he was fairly certain she wasn't because there was nothing under her T-shirt. "Are you wearing underwear?"

"No, but don't change the subject."

"I say we definitely change the subject," he said as he started to slide his T-shirt up and off her.

She grabbed onto his hands and stopped him, however, her hands gripping his tightly. "What do you want from me?" she demanded.

Well that was easy. "Everything."

Her chest rose and fell rapidly as she stared up at him. "That's not an answer."

He lifted a shoulder. "It's true. I want everything from you, Reese. I fell for you months ago and I don't see the point in fighting it."

"It's way too soon for this," she said waving her left-hand ring finger at him.

"Fine. It's too soon, but just keep it for now. We can make it official later."

She let out a short scream of frustration. "How is this so easy to you? I don't want to be someone you get engaged to just like with your last—"

"I never proposed to her. She talked about wanting to get married and then said we should shop for a ring. But I never *asked* her to marry me. I went along with it, and looking back I want to say I don't know why, but I do. I was just desperate to find someone who loved me. I was lonely and it didn't matter that she wasn't who I wanted. And then I met you, and was never so grateful to be single in my entire life. Because if I had been dating someone when I met you, I would've ended things with them."

She blinked once. Twice. "You're so perfect it's annoying."

He snort-laughed and lifted her up onto the countertop. "I am definitely not perfect. But I can keep pretending for as long as it takes."

"You cook, you don't care that I can be cranky, you agreed to meet my parents before we were even dating—"

"We were dating." Or heading that way.

"Maybe in your *mind*," she said on a laugh. "You're always thinking of other people. You give away so much money to those in need it defies reality. And you have a *fantastic* ass."

"I really feel like you should've started with my ass because it's one of my best features."

She reached around and pinched said ass. "You are *not* wrong. So okay, we can date, but maybe we don't put a label or anything—"

"We're absolutely putting a label on things. You are *mine*. I don't care if you want to be my girlfriend, my fiancée, my wife—"

She slapped her hand against his mouth again which just made him grin. "Stop it with that."

He licked her.

She yelped at the contact. "Gross."

"Yet it's not gross when I lick between your legs?"

Her eyes went heated at that. "Stop trying to distract me."

"Or...I can distract you with my mouth?" He finished what he'd started earlier with her shirt and tugged it up and over her head.

And sighed in pure appreciation to see all of her bared to him, her perfect breasts and tight brown nipples that were just begging for his mouth.

"When you look at me like that, it scares me," she whispered, more than a hint of vulnerability in her normally confident voice.

He snapped his eyes to hers. "Like what?"

"Like I'm the best Christmas present you've ever received."

Sighing, he laid his forehead against hers because despite the differences in the way they'd been raised, it was clear they'd both been lonely. "Why is that a bad thing?" he murmured.

"Because I'm terrified you're going to realize I'm not that great eventually. And it'll rip my heart out when you do."

"Ah, Reese. I'm sorry that someone made you feel not good enough." And he was pretty sure it was her goddamn parents. "But I'm not walking away. Words only go so far, but if you'll let me, I'll show you over and over how much you mean to me. I know we haven't known each other that long so I get your hesitation at this thing between us. But even in my wildest fantasies, I'd never even hoped for someone like you. Someone who will have my back—and someone who'd stab someone through the eye to keep me safe."

She gave him a soft smile. "I'd stab someone anywhere to keep you safe."

"Exactly. Just take a chance on us." Because he was putting his heart in her hands too.

"Okay. But if you break my heart...I might stab you too."

"Duly noted." He grinned as he leaned in, nipped her bottom lip between his teeth.

Just like that, she arched into him, wrapping her entire body around him as he leaned into her. He tugged his own shirt off, managing to take his mouth off hers for only a moment before they were kissing again.

He slid his fingers through the mass of her dark hair as he lifted her off the countertop, wanting to get somewhere a little flatter.

They barely made it to the stairs before he was just as naked and pushing inside her wet heat.

"Constantine," she moaned as he thrust inside her again, barely in control as her inner walls tightened around him.

And he loved when she said his full name. Especially when she was naked and he was inside her and she was crying out with a desperation that matched his own.

He couldn't even find his voice as he moved inside her again, not when his balls were pulled up so tight his own last name eluded him.

As she arched her back against him, her nipples brushing against his chest again, he felt the little ripple of her inner walls telling him how close she was. Since he was minutes away from embarrassing himself, he reached between their bodies and began teasing her clit.

She jerked against him, biting down on his lip as he increased his pressure. He knew she was close now which meant he wouldn't be embarrassing himself. Not today anyway.

"I'm almost there," she moaned out.

"Good," he growled. "You can come on my face later." Because he was absolutely obsessed with going down on her, with the way she rode his face or just burying his face between her legs.

Her entire body jolted at his words, and yeah, he knew she liked when he talked dirty. Could feel her inner walls clenching faster and faster.

He dipped a head to her breast, sucked hard on her tight nipple. And she jolted again.

"Maybe I'll take you up against my front window, give our neighbors a show," he murmured before he took her nipple between his teeth.

Aaaaand she started coming hard, so he let the wave of his sweep him away as well. Allowed himself to lose control as he climaxed inside her, until they were both out of breath and panting in the middle of his stairs.

Gently she ran her fingernails up and down his back, her smile sated and almost sleepy. "Do you really want to do it in front of your neighbors?"

Laughing lightly, he brushed his mouth against hers. "Hell. No. I would never share you with anyone. But I know you like it when I talk dirty."

She tightened around his half-hard cock and yep, he knew he'd hit the mark. Not that he'd doubted it. Not when it came to this woman who'd climbed right under his skin and was now a part of him.

Groaning, he forced himself to get up, mainly because he didn't want her getting sore on the stairs. Then he scooped her up and headed to his room—hopefully soon to be their room.

Because they still had time before their meeting and he was going to spend every second possible inside her or pleasuring her. Or both.

# Chapter 34

"It's too early to be here," Reese grumbled as she collapsed on one of the chairs at the conference room table.

"It's noon." Skye's tone was dry.

Yeah, well, Reese didn't care. She wanted to be back at Cash's place. Naked. Having orgasms. Eating chocolate cake. Maybe all at the same time. She didn't have to choose her pleasure at this point.

Cash strode into the room, looking more gorgeous than any mere mortal had a right to. His dark hair was tousled perfectly, the T-shirt he wore stretched across those perfect abs, chest...everything. And he was carrying a plate with a piece of Swedish chocolate cake on it.

She sat up straighter. "You're the best."

He simply grinned as he sat, kissed her on the top of her head.

"You can't bring any for the rest of us?" Elijah grumbled.

"Yeah," Skye added.

Rowan simply rolled his eyes.

"There's more in the kitchen for everyone. And I'm picking up another on the way home," he murmured to Reese.

And yep, she fell even harder. He knew the way to her heart—food. And orgasms. And food and orgasms together. Yeah, that sounded good—

"Okay, I'm going to just get to it," Skye started, cutting off Reese's thoughts as Colt strolled into the room and took one of the chairs. He was holding their dog C-4, with Hailey's corgi trotting behind them, happily panting.

"The DEA freaking loves us right now. That's the short of it. We handed them a big win and now we've got a favor in our back pocket. I want you all to take a few days off and regroup, and then we'll talk about new cases. We've had some roll in, but as of now Rowan is going to take over as lead until Hailey is back."

Reese glanced at Rowan, saluted him with her fork.

He just grinned, but the smile didn't reach his eyes. She wondered if it had something to do with the fact that Adalyn was conspicuously missing from the meeting.

"Where's Adalyn?" she asked because she'd never been able to keep her curiosity on lock. Probably why she liked hacking stuff.

Skye just gave her a look. "Somewhere else." Then she cleared her throat. "Anyway, to give you the long version of what happened, Alban Shehu's death has been ruled an accident. Or whatever. The mountain lion escaped, at least."

Reese let out a breath she hadn't realized she was holding. The animal might not have intentionally done it, but she'd likely saved her life and Reese would forever be grateful.

"Joelle has decided to quit and move somewhere warmer, but it sounds like Mila is going to give her a severance. She's horrified by what her husband did and I think she feels guilty for not knowing what was going on. And I think she knew about the extracurricular activities with some of the employees but chose to ignore it. But she didn't know about the drugs, that much the DEA is sure of. Ben Kingston is flipping on his suppliers but it doesn't matter at this point because they've got him dead to rights on two murders. The sheriff will do some time as well. Conroy might, but he's agreed to testify against his boss so I don't think he will. I think he'll end up in WITSEC. Oh, and the reason Ben killed that guy's nephew is because the man killed one of Kingston's employees, Wayne Thomas. The guy was a guide, but he was also helping Ben move product and got into it with one of the Albanians. Ben had told Mila that the guide had quit but apparently she didn't believe him. She'd called her girlfriend about it, which is why Detective Lippman was at the ranch when you," Skye said, looking at Rowan, "saw her in the stables. I'm sure more shit will come out but for now it seems like the DEA has things under control."

"What about the employee Lauren? The masseuse?"

"She quit too," Skye said. "And yes, she was having an affair with Ben Kingston as well. I think Mila is settling with her, giving her a severance."

"What about the Albanians? Do we need to worry about blowback?" Cash asked.

"I don't think so but I've called in a favor regardless. A very scary individual owes me a favor and he's let the Albanians know that if they come after anyone from the wellness center, they'll regret it."

"How scary?" Reese asked around a bite of food. She bit back a groan, but it was hard because this stuff was so good.

"He takes the heads of his enemies as a warning." The first words Colt had spoken were serious as he glanced at Reese. "And that's not hyperbole."

"Ah. Okay, then. So we can sleep soundly at night. Oh, whatever happened to Rae Brown?"

"She's back home and not under arrest or suspicion. The DEA is pretty certain that the Albanians killed her husband because he'd seen one of them. And as far as the wellness center, I have no idea if it will stay open or not. And I honestly don't care. Aubry Boyle's body has been sent home to her mother so at least she'll get closure. The details of your involvement have been kept to a minimum. As far as the official report goes, you were in the right place at the right time and took the right actions to stop your fellow guests from being murdered. Win-win for everyone."

"What about the whole 'plane landing on the highway' thing? Because you never really answered that."

Skye lifted an eyebrow. "You're nosy today."

Reese grinned. "All day, every day."

Colt cleared his throat before answering. "My wife is very impatient and convinced the pilot to land on the highway since the airport was trying to redirect us because of the snow. She told him if he did, Brooks would give him ten grand in cash. So."

Reese snickered. "How did Brooks respond to that?"

"He's so delirious now that Darcy gave birth that he didn't mind at all." And Skye looked smug about that.

"Oh my god! Why didn't you lead with that?" Rowan demanded. "Darcy had her baby already? Is she okay?" He'd become close with Brooks since coming on with Redemption Harbor even though they were in another state. Must be that whole military thing they had in common. But the man was tight with both Brooks and Savage, two of the founders.

"Everyone is healthy and happy, and for the record, I told him not to tell you because I knew you'd get distracted on the job. Feel free to call him after this meeting."

Rowan grumbled to himself, but as the meeting wrapped up, Reese turned to Cash and grinned. "Ready to get out of here?"

His gaze fell to her mouth, his eyes heating in an instant. "Yep."

"Are you guys grabbing lunch? I'm starving," Elijah said as he stood.

"Ah…" Reese cleared her throat.

Rowan clapped him on the shoulder. "I'll take you to lunch. Those two don't want company right now."

"Did someone say lunch?" Ezra stuck his head in the conference room. "I just polished off some cake but I'm starving. Tiago and B are here too. I know they're up to eat."

"Hey! That cake was for everyone." Skye stalked from the room, likely going in search of more food.

"And that's why I brought in multiple cakes," Cash murmured as he pulled her to her feet.

Reese linked her fingers through his, ignoring the banter of the others as the two of them snuck out. Much like they'd snuck away the night of Hailey and Jesse's wedding.

"Hey, have you told Jesse that we're together?" she asked as they reached the parking lot.

"Uh, no. I haven't even had time."

"Oh, well I told Easton and Hailey so I'm sure he knows anyway."

Cash blinked down at her. "You told Easton?"

"Yep. We're on a group text with Hailey and a couple others."

"How did I not know this?"

"Because I'm a woman of mystery."

Laughing, he pinned her up against his SUV. "I like that you're friends with my friends."

"And I like your dick so let's get out of here."

He let out a bark of laughter that soothed her soul, because she loved his laugh. Loved every single thing about him. And she just had to figure out a way to say the words without sounding stupid. She'd never told anyone she loved them other than her parents. Or her friends, but that was a different kind of love.

This was on another level. And considering the way he'd grown up, her instinct told her that she needed to be the one to open up first. She wanted him to know how special he was to her, that she valued everything about him.

That she wanted to create a life with him.

## Chapter 35

"So what's up?" Rowan stepped into his office, shut the door behind him and Skye. She'd told him she wanted to talk to him before they all headed out for food.

She set her plate of mostly eaten cake down on his desk and leaned against the front of it. "Just wanted to tell you how impressed I am with you. You really acted like a pro during this job."

"Is that what Adalyn told you?" She hadn't talked to him on the jet ride home, and then hadn't been at the meeting today. And he hated that he cared. He was supposed to hate her.

"In so many words. You know what she's like, a woman of few words. But what she didn't say spoke volumes. So you pulled your head out of your ass and did what needed to be done."

He nodded briefly, wondering where this was going. "I'm just glad we all survived and Aubry's mother will have closure."

Skye nodded, her expression grim. "I know, and I hate how often people go missing with no one to do anything about it..." Trailing off, she shook her head. "That's not why I called you in here. I've been talking with the others about onboarding some new people. If we do, I don't know that we'll need another office, but we are going to need a new team leader essentially. Especially since I think Hailey might not be pulling back exactly, but her priorities in life are going to change. I know I said that I want you as lead until she gets back…but I really want you to take on new responsibilities and a new leadership role in general."

Rowan nodded. "It's good to have a backup anyway. Things are always changing and we need to be adaptable to those changes."

"You sound exactly like my husband. Which means that you're right." She stared at him for a long moment and he felt as if he was under a microscope.

"What's that look for?"

"I'm sitting on some information and I'm debating on whether I should tell you or not," she said bluntly.

He rolled his eyes. "Tell me, don't tell me, it's fine."

"Now you're just annoying me." She stared at him for another long moment. "Do you know why Adalyn left the CIA?"

He looked away, shrugged.

"Fine, I'm going to tell you mainly because it's clear you don't. She resigned but she was going to be fired. Or maybe not fired, but they were eventually going to push her out. They would've found a reason. Or hell, set her up for something. She went after Bes Ali."

That got his attention. Rowan's head swiveled back toward Skye at the mention of the deceased Egyptian gunrunner. "What the hell are you talking about?"

"She went after him. At least that's the unofficial word."

"No, he died in a freak car accident." He'd read the report. Ali had run off the road while partying in Ibiza.

Skye lifted an eyebrow.

He stared at her. "Wait, are you serious? He was murdered and…are you saying that it *wasn't* company sanctioned?"

"That's exactly what I'm saying. She took matters into her own hands and got revenge. Or what some would call justice." Skye sniffed indignantly and there was no doubt she considered what Adalyn had done as justice.

"Who was her backup?"

"No one, as far as I know."

He sat back in his chair, beyond stunned as he digested the information. "They could've arrested her for that. Brought her up on a whole lot of charges. Or just thrown her in a hole somewhere and left her to rot." Because Ali had been a Company asset, someone deeply embedded with a terrorist group they were trying to keep tabs on.

Skye lifted a shoulder. "I don't know for sure that she did it, but...she did. And she pissed off some powerful people in the process. Made enemies."

He sat down in one of his chairs, scrubbed a hand over his face. "I thought she just walked away after her work with us and didn't look back." But he should have known better. Because Hailey wouldn't have invited Adalyn to the wedding otherwise.

"You thought she didn't give a crap about your guys, huh?" Skye shook her head and straightened as she picked up her leftover cake.

"I'm..."

"An idiot? Yeah, I know. Anyway, now you know the truth. Won't matter because she's going to be working with me, but I wanted the air to be clear for the future in case your paths ever crossed." She left him alone after that, his door shutting with a soft click behind her.

He continued sitting there as he digested the truth. Needing to talk to Adalyn, he pulled out his phone and was surprised when she answered on the second ring.

"What's up?"

"Hey, I...are you in town?" he asked.

"Yeah, for a couple more days."

"Can we get together and talk?"

She was silent for a long moment, then cursed. "Ah, hell. Skye talked to you, didn't she?"

He didn't respond.

Which she clearly took as a yes. "You know what, Rowan? No, we can't meet up. You can eat a dick." She ended the call before he could respond, and when he tried to call her back it went straight to voicemail.

Which sounded about right.

# EPILOGUE

*One month later*

"You're being cagey," Cash murmured as he pulled her close, pressing her up against his front door. He wanted to ask her to move in with him, but was trying to take it slow with Reese. Things between them were perfect and they'd worked two more short jobs since the Montana one.

"Not cagey." She smiled up at him, her green eyes bright. "Just excited to give you your birthday present."

He blinked in surprise. She'd taken him out to eat tonight—and sneakily paid for their dinner—then they'd gone walking along the bay and little shops downtown. Everything was close to his place so they'd been able to walk home and enjoy the coming spring air. And more importantly, he'd gotten some much needed alone time with her. "You know it's my birthday?"

"Yup. Hailey told me. And you're definitely getting lucky."

He quickly unlocked the door and shoved it open, making her laugh. And—

"Surprise!" The lights flipped on as most or all of their friends yelled from his living room. The place had been decorated with a gigantic balloon arch, streamers, and there was a table filled with presents.

Laughing, he looked down at Reese who was grinning up widely at him. She might as well have punched him right in the heart. No one had ever thrown him a surprise party. Or a birthday party at all. Sure, he'd gone out with friends over the years but this was different. His parents had never given a shit about his birthday, then in foster care, forget about it.

"Did I surprise you?" she whispered as Hailey and Jesse strode over to hug him.

"Definitely." He kissed her hard before he hugged his friends—who were finally back from their honeymoon.

Then he found himself face-to-face with Easton, who gave him another big hug. "Happy birthday, man."

"Thanks." Feeling overwhelmed, he took the glass of champagne someone put into his hand and greeted the next person who approached.

Reese hadn't gone far, thankfully, and slid right up next to him, tucking herself against him as they talked with their friends, some who'd become more like family in a short span.

The party went by in a blur, hours passing when it only felt like minutes, and he found himself barely containing his emotions. Something that normally took no effort at all. He was used to putting on a mask. He'd had to in order to survive. And then he'd gotten so used to it that it became part of who he was—the laid-back guy with the easy smile.

As he went searching for Reese, he felt anything other than laid-back. She'd disappeared a few minutes ago to "find more cake" and he found that even a few minutes separated from her was too much.

"So was it a good birthday?" Jesse clapped him on the shoulder as he strode into the foyer, planning to make his way to the kitchen.

"Ah, yeah. Best birthday I've ever had."

"You really didn't know?"

"Nope. Which is a little terrifying that she kept it a secret."

Jesse just laughed. "She's been a little manic planning it. She made it clear that if anyone told you, accidentally or otherwise, they'd lose a body part or two."

That sounded like Reese. "How is it being back?"

"Good. The honeymoon was amazing but I'm ready to start our life, to settle in."

"So you're really moving here, huh?"

"Yep."

"Good. I've got some properties I've been looking at scooping up. I've got some ideas."

"Of course you do. Whatever it is, you know I'm in." Jesse shook his head. "Come on, let's find our ladies."

Yeah, Jesse was just as bad as Cash was. The man had just spent weeks wrapped up with his wife, but didn't like being separated for even a few minutes.

Something Cash understood.

He found Reese talking with Hailey and Easton in his kitchen, empty dessert plates in front of them at the island top as they laughed about something.

Reese's jet-black hair was down tonight in a waterfall of soft waves. She'd worn a skintight red dress he'd been dreaming about peeling from her body from the moment she'd walked through his front door. Her legs were crossed, causing her dress to ride up slightly, showing off skin he wanted to trace over with his mouth and every other part of him. He basically wanted to imprint on her with an obsession that should scare him.

He moved in behind her and she immediately swiveled her stool, looking up at him as if she could devour him.

"Hey, birthday boy," she whispered, heat in her voice.

He was vaguely aware of the others heading out of the kitchen and he was glad because he wanted a few moments alone with her. "Hey, yourself. And thank you for this. This is the best gift anyone's ever given me."

She turned fully toward him and spread her legs as wide as her dress would allow. "Really?"

Leaning down, he brushed his lips over hers. "Definitely."

"Well it's going to get even better when everyone leaves. Because we'll be naked," she whispered. "Also, I need to tell you something." Something about her tone had him straightening.

"What?"

"Well...as I'm saying this, I'm realizing I probably should have waited until it was just the two of us, but screw it. I love you, Constantine. I have for a while, but I didn't want to mess up the dynamic between us because things have been so perfect it's kind of scary. And don't feel like you have to say—"

"I love you too." He crushed his mouth to hers before she could continue, teasing his tongue with hers as the purest sense of joy enveloped him. She loved him, the real him. Not because of his wealth, but him. The man. "And you're going to be my wife," he growled, pulling back only slightly.

She stared up at him, eyes wide. "Is that...your idea of a proposal?"

Okay so she wasn't saying no. He pulled the ring that he'd been carrying around the last two weeks from his back pocket and slid it onto her finger. "Nope because I'm not asking."

She blinked, but then her mouth kicked up into a huge smile. "You're kinda bossy."

"I am."

"I kinda like it," she whispered.

"I know." He nipped her bottom lip and had to order his body to stay under control when all he wanted to do was take her right on the countertop. But he could be patient. Maybe. Probably. "Can we kick everyone out?" he whispered.

Laughing, she shook her head as she pushed at his chest. "No way, but I promise to wear this and only this," she said, holding out her left-hand ring finger as she stood, "later, while you bend me over this countertop."

He groaned and pulled her close. "Fine, but we're having a short engagement."

"You're very sure of yourself, birthday boy."

No, but he was sure of her. Of them. He kissed her again, this time softer and full of promise of the night to come.

Finally she pulled back, her eyes bright. "I bet we can plan a wedding even faster than Hailey and Jesse. We can hire Jasmine and let her do her magic."

"She's already on standby," he confessed.

At his words, she let out the sweetest laugh. "I do love a man who's prepared."

And he kissed her again. Because she was the only woman he'd ever loved and he was damn sure that he was going to be the only man she ever loved.

# Acknowledgments

As always, I'm grateful to a host of people! Thank you to Julia for editing, Tammy and Shelley for proofreading, Jaycee for my fabulous cover, and Sarah for all the things. To the best writer pups, Jack and Piper, thank you for forcing me to get out in the sunshine every day. I'm also incredibly grateful to my mom whose help allows me to focus on writing more. For my readers, you all are the best! I'm truly, truly grateful that you keep reading my books and asking for more.

# About the Author

Katie Reus® is the *USA Today* bestselling author of the Red Stone Security series, the Ancients Rising series and the Redemption Harbor series. She fell in love with romance at a young age thanks to books she pilfered from her mom's stash. Years later she loves reading romance almost as much as she loves writing it.

However, she didn't always know she wanted to be a writer. After changing majors many times, she finally graduated summa cum laude with a degree in psychology. Not long after that she discovered a new love. Writing. She now spends her days writing paranormal romance and sexy romantic suspense.

# Complete Booklist

***Ancients Rising***
Ancient Protector
Ancient Enemy
Ancient Enforcer
Ancient Vendetta
Ancient Retribution
Ancient Vengeance
Ancient Sentinel
Ancient Warrior
Ancient Guardian

***Darkness Series***
Darkness Awakened
Taste of Darkness
Beyond the Darkness
Hunted by Darkness
Into the Darkness
Saved by Darkness
Guardian of Darkness
Sentinel of Darkness

A Very Dragon Christmas
Darkness Rising

***Deadly Ops Series***
Targeted
Bound to Danger
Chasing Danger
Shattered Duty
Edge of Danger
A Covert Affair

***Endgame Trilogy***
Bishop's Knight
Bishop's Queen
Bishop's Endgame

***Holiday With a Hitman Series***
How the Hitman Stole Christmas
A Very Merry Hitman

***MacArthur Family Series***
Falling for Irish
Unintended Target
Saving Sienna

***Moon Shifter Series***
Alpha Instinct
Lover's Instinct
Primal Possession
Mating Instinct
His Untamed Desire

Avenger's Heat
Hunter Reborn
Protective Instinct
Dark Protector
A Mate for Christmas

***O'Connor Family Series***
Merry Christmas, Baby
Tease Me, Baby
It's Me Again, Baby
Mistletoe Me, Baby

***Red Stone Security Series®*stone**
No One to Trust
Danger Next Door
Fatal Deception
Miami, Mistletoe & Murder
His to Protect
Breaking Her Rules
Protecting His Witness
Sinful Seduction
Under His Protection
Deadly Fallout
Sworn to Protect
Secret Obsession
Love Thy Enemy
Dangerous Protector
Lethal Game
Secret Enemy
Saving Danger
Guarding Her

Deadly Protector
Danger Rising
Protecting Rebel

### *Redemption Harbor® Series*
Resurrection
Savage Rising
Dangerous Witness
Innocent Target
Hunting Danger
Covert Games
Chasing Vengeance

### *Redemption Harbor® Security*
Fighting for Hailey
Fighting for Reese
Fighting for Adalyn
Fighting for Magnolia

### *Sin City Series (the Serafina)*
First Surrender
Sensual Surrender
Sweetest Surrender
Dangerous Surrender
Deadly Surrender

### *Verona Bay Series*
Dark Memento
Deadly Past
Silent Protector

***Linked books***
Retribution
Tempting Danger

***Non-series Romantic Suspense***
Running From the Past
Dangerous Secrets
Killer Secrets
Deadly Obsession
Danger in Paradise
His Secret Past

***Paranormal Romance***
Destined Mate
Protector's Mate
A Jaguar's Kiss
Tempting the Jaguar
Enemy Mine
Heart of the Jaguar

Made in the USA
Middletown, DE
29 March 2024